THE COST OF BLISS

First paperback edition October 2023.

Cover design by Books and Moods

ISBN 979-8-218-25632-6 (Paperback)

For Evelynn Ray,

May you always find the sunshine.

1

I am named after a character in a book I've never read. Some people are named after their grandparents, famous people, real historical figures, or they have their own names that only belong to them and no one else. Well, not me. I have to share my name with someone who isn't real, and whom I'm sure did a lot more impressive things in her world than I'm doing in mine. Jane, after *Jane Eyre,* was my dad's idea. When I asked him about it when I was little, he said, "Your name is to remind you that you can overcome." Overcome what, I have no clue.

Dad works at the local museum and is obsessed with history, art, and literature. He's the smartest person I know. I'm pretty sure he's a curator or something. Though now that I'm thinking about it, he's never actually told me what his exact job title is. I should probably ask him sometime.

Dad's always telling me and my little sister about the interesting, expensive, and extremely old and boring artifacts they have on display at the museum. Not that my little sister ever listens to what he says. She's like a little tornado who never sits still - even if you glued her legs to a chair. She's also named after a book character. Scout, from *To Kill a Mockingbird*. Dad says her name fits her personality perfectly; that's she's living up to her name. I wouldn't know. I've never read *that* book either.

Now, before you think I've never read anything *ever*, I'll have you know that I get all A's in school (okay, and the occasional B). I make the best grades out of nearly everyone in the eighth grade at Blossom View Middle School. There's a lot of students, too, so that's even more impressive when you think about it. It's easy to get lost and difficult to stand out. It's a good thing I'm a hard worker.

I think about this as I walk up the long, winding hill to our house from the bus stop. I wish I didn't have to take the bus to and from school every day. But since Scout is only four years old, she's still asleep when I leave in the morning. Mom says it just makes more sense for me to take the bus. I don't mind it too terribly, but all my friends carpool with each other. They always look like they're having so much fun getting dropped off and picked up together every day. They usually have overly sugary coffee drinks with them in the morning, and then talk about asking to get dropped off at the mall after school. I wonder if they ever wish I was with them . . . I certainly do. I've complained to my mom about this often, but she pretends she doesn't hear me whenever I bring it up. I guess it's just not worth the fight – for now. Pretty soon I'll be in high school, and she'll *have* to let me go and do things with them then, right? I mean, my social livelihood depends on it.

As I trudge up the steps to the house, I notice a piece of paper taped on the front door. We've been getting these papers on our door pretty often over the last couple of months, but I have no clue what they are, nor do I really care. I take the note off the door, not bothering to read it, and walk into the foyer of the house. As I do, I try my best to avoid tripping over the moving boxes we've stacked there.

I love our house. It's a gorgeous three stories, with five bedrooms, three bathrooms, and our very own media room in the finished basement. The rest of the houses in our neighborhood are very similar to one another, but ours is unique because it was one of the first houses built around here. It has beautiful columns holding up the front porch, exquisite landscaping with flower beds galore, and a gazebo in the backyard with a bright yellow porch swing that's perfect for escaping from Scout. I've convinced her the gazebo is haunted.

When my parents told me we were moving, I was heartbroken. Am still heartbroken. We're not moving very far, just to another house on the other side of town. But this new house only has four bedrooms and two full bathrooms, which means I'll have to share a bathroom with Scout. The very thought is almost too much to bear.

"Hey, Mom," I say as I walk into the kitchen.

"Hey, hun," she replies, as she places a plate gently into a box of dishware. "How was school?"

"Fine," I answer, like always. "There was another paper on the door," I say as I hand the slip to her. As I do, I notice her usually pleasant expression falter. She takes the paper, frowning slightly.

"What's wrong?" I inquire. Her face immediately rights itself as she gives her head a slight shake.

"Nothing. Just a little lost in thought is all," she says. "Why don't you go put your stuff away and start on your homework? Maybe see if Scout wants to play?"

Hard pass. Scout's version of playing is seeing how loud she can scream before our parents say something or I burst an eardrum. But I just nod in assent, still wondering what she was thinking when I handed her that paper; why it was different from the other ones we've gotten on the door lately. I leave the kitchen, walk down the hall, and climb up the stairs toward my bedroom. Scout hears me approaching and pops her little blonde head out of her room.

"Janey! Want to play teacher with me?" she asks imploringly. She looks at me expectantly, hoping against hope that I'll jump up and down with joy at the prospect of playing with her. As if.

"No, I played student all day, so I'm all set. I have homework to do anyway. Just play by yourself." I turn away but sneak a glance at her over my shoulder.

She backs into her room with her head hung low and shuts her door. I feel a slight pang of guilt, but quickly clear it from my head. She'll be fine. I can play with her tomorrow. I go into my bedroom, close my own door, and throw my backpack onto my unmade bed. I fall, exhausted from the day, into my armchair. As I look around at my room, I think that it could use a makeover.

All my furniture is old. The white paint is peeling from my bed and the dresser, my desk is lopsided, and my bedding still looks like a ten-year-old picked it out. Of course, ten-year-old *me* did pick it out. It's a bright hot pink thing with zebra print . . . just like everything was when I was ten. It's definitely time for an update. I think I'll ask Mom and Dad if they can get me some new furniture for the new house. Surely, it's normal to get new furniture every few years or so. I'm pretty sure my friend, Lexi, gets new stuff every single year. She lives right down the street from us, and they always have new *everything*. Fancy china, those beds that have remotes so they can move, and a pool in their backyard with its own cascading waterfall!

I bet we could have all new stuff if we wanted, but my parents are pretty frugal if you ask me. It's odd. They'll say yes to some things, but no to things that I think they should say yes to. For instance, a few months ago around Christmas time, I asked Mom when we were going to take a vacation, since all my friends were going on trips for the holidays. It took her a while to respond, but in the end she just said that the holidays were for family, then promptly changed the subject. Then later, when we were opening gifts, I got everything I asked for – name brand shoes, clothes, a new curling iron, and a trampoline for the backyard!

I've wondered about this a lot over the past year or so. Dad makes plenty of money at the museum, seeing as how we own this really nice house. I suspect they're just saving for mine and Scout's college funds, but since I'm so smart I'm sure I'll earn a lot of scholarships. They won't even *need* to pay for my college! *That's* how I'll convince them to buy me new furniture. If they say no to my request, I'll just tell them that they can use the money from my college fund.

I stand up, stretch my arms a bit, then settle into my desk chair. I dig out my math workbook from my backpack, sighing as I remember how many problems Mrs. Gentry assigned us to complete tonight. It's not difficult work – just plotting some transformations - but it sure is tedious. I work fervently for about an hour when I hear the garage door open and the familiar sounds of Dad getting home from work.

As if on cue, I hear Scout's door open and the sound of her bounding down the stairs to greet him. I know better, though. Dad doesn't like to be bothered too much when he gets home. He likes to go straight to take a shower and then joins us right when dinner is ready. Scout doesn't understand the importance of a routine yet. She'll learn soon enough, I expect, though she won't start kindergarten until the year after next since she'll miss the age cut-off for this upcoming school year.

Scout stays at home with Mom during the day, since Mom doesn't work. She doesn't need to and she doesn't want to, as she often reminds us. She always says that she doesn't want to miss her kids' childhoods – that they're much too important to hand over to a daycare. I've always admired this mindset. When I have kids, there's no way that I'll send them to *strangers* to be raised. People who send their kids to daycare must not love their kids as much as my parents love me and Scout. It's a shame, really.

I finally finish the mountain of math problems, and place my workbook safe and sound back into my backpack as Mom calls up to me that dinner is ready. We *always* eat dinner together as a family, and Dad makes each of us take turns talking about our days. Seeing as how

Scout usually takes up all the breath in the room with what she did that day – usually it's whatever happened on that pony princess show she watches like a maniac – I typically don't have to talk too much.

As I make my way down the stairs, something feels different. It's like someone really has sucked all the breath out of the room. Though somehow, I don't think it was Scout. I decide not to mention whatever it is I am feeling about this change of energy in the house. For whatever reason, I feel like those pieces of paper on the door are more important than I originally thought. But I won't say anything just yet. I don't want Mom to get upset, and I need her in a good mood if I have any chance of getting new furniture.

When I reach the dining room, I realize that I am starving. I take a glance at the table and see that Mom has prepared homemade meatloaf, creamy mashed potatoes with cheese, green beans with bacon, and soft bread rolls with butter. *Delicious*. I'm the first one to be seated at the table, so I have to wait until everyone else makes their way over before I can start eating. I wish they'd hurry up. Scout comes in next and sits in her booster chair, looking as bubbly as ever. *I guess she got over me saying no to playing*, I think.

I had quickly forgotten about the strange feeling I got on the stairs but am instantly reminded of it when my parents come into the room and sit down. They're not acting particularly strange or odd. Dad is wearing what he always wears after work: gray joggers, an old t-shirt, and a soft smile that just barely reaches his bright blue eyes. Mom is still wearing her apron over her usual t-shirt and leggings, with her dark brown hair clipped up in a messy bun. On the outside, everyone is behaving quite normally. But something is off, though I still can't quite put my finger on it. We start eating.

"Scout," Dad says, looking at her with delight, "why don't you tell us about your day? Did you have any highs, lows, or buffaloes?"

Ugh, I think while internally rolling my eyes, *why does this family call anything funny that happens a buffalo? It doesn't even make sense.* But Scout jumps right in, talking a mile a minute, not bothering to question the absurdity of the notion.

"I got to play with my new dolls that Mommy got for me, so that was really fun, but then when Jane got home she wouldn't play school with me so that made me really sad. Nothing weird or funny happened. Oh wait, Mr. Perry came to the house when Mommy was taking a bath, and he knocked on the door a lot. That was weird," she says without taking a breath.

We all stop eating and look at her. Mr. Perry is a family friend of ours. Dad went to college with his son, James, but since James moved away, we've always invited Mr. Perry to come to the house for holidays, birthdays, things like that. He hasn't ever come by unannounced or uninvited, at least that I know of.

"Mr. Perry came by the house?" Dad asks her, a glob of mashed potatoes falling from his fork that had been on its way to his mouth.

"Yep!" Scout says enthusiastically. "I didn't open the door because Mommy told me never to open the door by myself." Dad looks at Mom with what I can only describe as concern in his eyes. I've never seen that look from him before. *What is going on?*

Mom gives an almost imperceptible shake of her head in Dad's direction that seems to communicate to him that she'll explain later. I sure do wish she would explain now. Aren't I old enough to be a part of adult conversations? I'm mature enough to handle it. But I don't say anything right then. I still need to ask them about getting me new furniture for the move, and I don't want them to say no because I butted in where they think I shouldn't. So I pretend I don't notice the awkward exchange between them.

"Jane, you're next," Dad says, effectively moving the conversation along like nothing happened.

"Well," I begin, "Paisley got a new puppy." Paisley is another one of my friends. She, Lexi, Ashlynn, and I have been super close friends since we were in preschool. The four of us are basically inseparable. "It's like a husky or something," I continue, "so I'm sure it's going to be really big. She showed us pictures and it's really cute . . . so I guess that was my high of the day."

I pause, thinking quickly about how I want to bring up my room makeover. I look down at my plate and push around my green beans as I speak.

"Oh, and Ashlynn's parents got her a brand new desk. You know, for high school, since we'll have so much more homework." I sneak a glance up at my parents. They're both eating their meal but look like they're listening, so I go on.

"I was thinking maybe I could get a new desk, too, so I can be ready for next year. Then while we're at it, we could get me a new bed and dresser so they'll all match!" Mom and Dad both look at each other again, doing that thing they do where they seem to talk to one another without actually speaking.

Dad speaks to me first, still giving Mom a sideways glance as if he's making sure he's saying the right thing as he says it.

"I think the furniture you have is just fine. Maybe we can talk about it more in a couple of years. It's important to get all the life you can out of stuff like that, because it can be pretty expensive to get all new ones."

"Well, I was thinking that we could just use the money from my college fund to pay for it," I say eagerly, "since we know I'll get a lot of scholarships!"

"Jane, that's not what college funds are for," Mom explains gently. "We can't just take money out of them whenever we want. Your dad said your furniture is fine and I agree. We can talk about it in a couple of years. We need to get settled into the new house first."

I know by her kind yet definitive tone that the discussion is over, so I don't press it. But my mind is still reeling. I still don't understand how they will get me *some* things, but other things – that I could actually use to be productive – are a resounding N-O. I look back down at my plate, disappointed. I'm sure they notice my face, but no one says anything. In fact, no one says much the rest of the meal.

It's a bit strange that Dad isn't telling us about *his* day. He's usually full of stories about the visitors of the museum that day, rattling off fun facts about an artifact, or telling us really bad jokes to get us to laugh. Tonight, though, he just seems solemn. But I have no clue as to why.

We finish our dinner then bring our plates to the kitchen sink for Mom to wash later. Scout and I head to the living room for our usual Tuesday night family routine of watching reruns of Jeopardy, when I notice that Mom and Dad didn't follow us. I can hear their muffled voices from a slight distance, meaning they went to their bedroom to have a private conversation. Which, of course, is *all* of their conversations. They never seem to talk to one another in front of us, unless it's about the family, or little trivial things like whether or not the lawn needs mowing.

There's something extra odd about their behavior tonight – the paper on the door, the concern in Mom's eyes, Dad's lack of enthusiastic chatter – that draws me to their closed bedroom door. I slide silently along the hardwood in sock feet, crouching low so I can hear their conversation through the crack between the door and the floor. I catch Dad's clear and calm whisper in the middle of a sentence.

"– another notice? I thought we had more time?"

"I thought we did, too," Mom whispers back, "but he says he needs us out by the end of the week."

Needs us out? Who needs us out? Out of where? None of it makes sense.

I can hear Dad's voice change to the soft tone he uses when Mom is upset.

"Juliette, something else happened today." He takes a sharp breath in and sighs, "Paul called me into his office today. They're downsizing. Immediately. I don't have a job anymore."

My heart sinks into my gut. Dad lost his job? But he loves it at the museum! Why would they want to get rid of him?

There's a long pause. I imagine Mom holding her hands to her mouth, Dad gently pulling her in for an embrace.

"What . . . *what* are we going to do?" Mom asks panicky. "Mr. Johnson was adamant that the only reason he was letting us into the new place was because you had stable employment. He knows Paul. He's obviously going to find out if he doesn't already know!"

"I know," Dad continues gently, sounding like he's trying to calm her down. "We're going to have to come up with something. Even if he still lets us come, without a job there's no way we could afford it anyways. But we can talk about it more tonight. Come on, I don't want the girls to get suspicious."

That's my cue. I stand up so fast I see stars for half a second, then race up the hall as quickly as I can without slipping. I fall haphazardly onto the sectional in the living room, feeling relief that neither of them caught me. I regain my breath quietly as my parents walk in. I look down and notice that Scout is playing with a doll she left in here yesterday, completely oblivious to everything that just transpired. I doubt she even noticed anything strange at all.

She has no reason for concern. I, on the other hand, have many.

2

I lie wide awake in my bed, my brain refusing to stop buzzing with all that happened tonight. After my parents walked into the living room, I waited with bated breath to see if they would tell us what had happened. But they didn't. They acted completely normal as if nothing out of the ordinary had occurred in the last decade, let alone the last couple of hours. We watched our Jeopardy, ate our usual butter pecan ice cream, said our goodnights, then went to bed. There wasn't a peep about Dad losing his job, us needing to be 'out' by the end of the week, or this mystery 'Mr. Johnson' person who evidently has a lot of leverage into where we're allowed to live and how much it costs.

Then the thing that has been bothering me the most comes to the forefront of my mind. *Why is it all such a secret?* I can handle being told important things. They should know that. Aren't they always telling me how mature I am for my age and how well I present myself to strangers? I understand why they wouldn't want to tell Scout, since she's so little. But why don't they trust *me?*

In the morning, I expect Mom and Dad to sit me down at the breakfast table and tell me everything. That doesn't happen. Neither of them says a word about any of it, other than Mom telling me I need to get going on cleaning out my closet so we can start packing up my stuff. But nothing about the urgency of our new timeline or why Dad is still home for breakfast when he should be at work already.

As I make my way down the hill of our neighborhood to the bus stop, I find myself becoming more and more frustrated and confused. My thoughts are going a million miles an hour, growing more and more anxious with every step. I barely notice there's already someone standing next to the stop sign. It's a boy in my grade: Preston Miller. He lives in the neighborhood across the street, a small apartment complex that's been there since the Stone Age of the 1980s. The buildings are dirty, all the cars look like they belong in a scrap yard, and it's a frequent destination for our local police force.

Preston greets me like he always does.

"Hey, Princess Jane."

He doesn't mean this endearingly. My last name is Prince, and Preston thinks that because we live in ValleyRidge, I'm some stuck up, entitled royalty-like figure. Therefore, Princess Jane became my nickname when he met me last year. I honestly don't see what's so special about our neighborhood, other than how gorgeous our houses are. I mean, it's not like we drink out of diamond-encrusted goblets or have our own personal chauffeurs, or housekeepers. Okay, Ashlynn's family has a driver who takes them places, but my family doesn't. And I guess Paisley's family has a lady that cleans their house every Thursday, but they, and I, are just normal people.

I roll my eyes at him but don't say anything. My mind is too preoccupied to produce a witty comeback right now. I then stare at my shoes, trying my best to process all that happened last night. It doesn't help that my brain is foggy from getting a lot less sleep than I normally do.

"How was the carriage ride down to the lowly bus stop this morning?" he pesters.

Carriage ride?! My dad just lost his job and didn't even tell me.

"What? Now you're too good to talk to me today? Typical ValleyRidge girl," he continues.

I'm about to unleash every insult I can think of at him when I look up and see him smirking at me with amusement, leaning casually against the stop sign. I'm not sure why, but this seems to calm me down a bit. He just wants to get a reaction from me. I take a deep breath and remind myself that Preston's not a bad guy... he's just a really annoying guy who could do with a quality haircut.

His dirty blonde hair lies scraggly over his eyes, and he keeps having to move it out of the way with a flick of his head or ruffling it with his hands. He's wearing the same pair of hole-ridden jeans he wears seventy-five percent of the time, a plain t-shirt, and sneakers that have seen better days. On his left shoulder is a red canvas backpack with a broken strap. I don't judge him (well, not outwardly) for not having very nice things. He lives in the Oakwood apartments. It's pretty obvious they can't afford very much. It's not Preston's fault, but surely he could do a bit more about his dirty clothes and broken backpack...and a haircut costs, what? Twenty bucks?

I stare at him for a second, then ultimately choose to take the high road and play along.

"Actually, it was a little bit bumpy today but it got me here safely, so I can't complain."

He grins at me, then looks away as he responds, "Well, you don't have much to complain about so I'm sure it wouldn't take much to make that happen."

I pause, thinking of the implications of what he just said. But it soon leaves my mind as our bus pulls up to the stop. For the entire ride to school, my thoughts drift back to the conversation I overheard last night between my parents. When are they planning on telling me about it? What will I say when they do? What job is Dad going to get? Where will we live if we can't live in the new house? Why did Mr. Perry coming over make them so nervous?

We arrive at school and I hop off the bus, relieved to see that Ashlynn, Paisley, and Lexi are waiting for me in the courtyard outside. I wonder if I should tell them about what happened last night. *No, I think. I don't have all the facts yet. And if it gets out that my dad lost his job, the rumors will start and never end, especially if Paisley knows. That girl doesn't know when to stop talking.* I walk over to where they stand. With their typical coffee cups in hand, they chatter nonstop about people in our class. Who said what, who has a crush on who, did you *see* what she's wearing today? They hardly notice I'm standing right in front of them.

There's finally a break in their conversation and Ashlynn turns slightly to greet me with a smile. Ashlynn and I have always been closer than the others. Paisley and Lexi tend to gravitate toward each other in the same way, but the four of us make a pretty solid friend group. I like it this way, because with four people, it's easy to have at least *one* person who wants to be around you that day.

"Jane, you *have* to hear this," Paisley says excitedly with a bright smile as she finally notices me. Her flaming red hair is tied up in a high ponytail, complete with her signature green bow sitting right at the top of her head. "Guess who Lexi just told us she has a CRUSH on?!" she continues animatedly.

This isn't breaking news. Lexi *always* has a crush on someone. And guess what? It *never* works out. She's never even had a real boyfriend, but she sure does talk about every . . . single . . . boy . . . in the school. A lot. All the time! I've always thought that it would be better for her to actually go up and talk *to* them instead of just talking *about* them to us. But what do I know? I've never had a boyfriend either, but I've never really sought one out, anyhow. I really don't care one bit who Lexi's newest obsession is, but I indulge them as always.

"Who is it?" I ask with forced enthusiasm and a crazy wide smile that hopefully conveys I'm much more interested in this than I actually am.

"Preston Miller!" Paisley exclaims.

"Shhhhhh!" Lexi says quickly, giggling and attempting to place her hands over Paisley's mouth. "Do you want everyone in a five-mile radius to hear you?"

My stomach flutters a bit when Paisley says his name, which takes me by surprise. Why should *I* care that Lexi has a crush on Preston? Preston and I are not even remotely close to being friends. And anyway, he doesn't seem to be Lexi's type.

"Oh, really?" I say to Lexi. "Why Preston, of all people?" I try to say this casually but can't ignore the accusatory tone that my voice involuntarily expresses. Thankfully, no one notices.

"He's really cute! His long hair that he's always flipping on his head is so hot, and he's kind of got this poor-boy charm that I just can't get over. Like I bet he'd just fall right in love with me if I bought him some decent kicks," Lexi explains why eyeing Preston across the lawn.

Her comment really rubs me the wrong way. Like, I don't care about Preston, I really don't; but the fact that she just said she could pretty much *buy* his affection so easily is disgusting to me. Does she really think he's that shallow? That he'll just follow her around like a lost puppy dog if she offered him expensive things *just* because his family lives in Oakwood? Gross.

My disdain for her comment must show on my face because Lexi and Paisley are looking at me like I grew horns. I immediately correct my expression into its usual look of feigned interest for their pettiness. I guess it mostly works because when Ashlynn changes the topic onto how much she hates her English teacher, Paisley and Lexi jump right into the gossip. At last, the bell rings, and as we walk toward the door into school, Ashlynn makes me slow down so we can talk without the other two overhearing.

"Is everything okay? You're acting kind of weird," Ashlynn says. I'm not sure what to tell her. I trust Ashlynn, but I also know that she can just as easily spread rumors as Paisley can, and I don't want to take the risk of something getting out and ruining my reputation. I'm supposed to have everything all together – all of the time. So I don't take the chance.

"Yeah, I just didn't sleep super well last night. That math homework took me forever – Scout kept distracting me – so I didn't get to bed until super late," I say nonchalantly. That works. It wasn't a *complete* lie. To Ashlynn's credit, she doesn't question this. She's still eyeing me a bit suspiciously as we walk down the hall to our first period history class, but she doesn't say anything further.

The rest of the day, I find it difficult to focus. My unexpected defensive thoughts for Preston Miller are interlaced with renewed worry about my parents' conversation from last night. Somehow, in the light of day, it's more concerning than when I first heard it. I don't think whatever is wrong would be as big of a deal if they would just *tell* me what is happening. I know my parents love and care about me, but they're treating me like I'm too fragile to handle the truth.

"Jane! Hello…? Are you in there?" Ashlynn snaps at me, with her voice and her fingers, waking me from my daze. My head snaps towards her, and I remember that she was telling me how unfair her mom had been for not letting her go to a high school party the weekend before last. I guess I didn't respond quickly enough to her, and she noticed that I wasn't listening.

"Yeah, of course I'm here," I start. "Sorry, I don't know what's wrong with me today. I just feel off." We're at lunch, sitting at our usual table in the back right corner of the cafeteria.

Even though we don't have assigned seats, everyone always sits at the same tables every day. In the few seconds after my lame excuse, I glance out at the spacious, high-ceilinged space, and notice the different groups. The football players always sit fifteen people to an 8-person table; the band geeks tend to split up and only sit with the people that play their same instrument; the theatre kids are obnoxiously loud at their table in the center; and then there's us. I'm not entirely sure what our group of four would be called. We're not particularly popular, but by no means are we *un*popular either. Everyone seems to like us, though, so I genuinely wonder what everyone else says when they talk about us.

Then I notice Preston. For the past couple of years that I've known him, I never bothered to pay attention to what group he belongs to. He's sitting with a mish mash of people in the table closest to the gym: one guy I know is in band, another's on the basketball team, and the others – I have no idea who they are, but they don't look like they would *ever* belong in the same group. Interesting.

I poke at my dry, flavorless spaghetti on its styrofoam tray as Ashlynn yammers to Lexi and Paisley. They sat down right after I spoke, saving me from Ashlynn's interrogation about my odd behavior today. When lunch ends, I get up quickly, toss my uneaten food in the trash can, then head to my Advanced Robotics class. This is good. None of my friends are in this class, so I can act as 'off' as I want.

The rest of the afternoon goes by quickly, and when the bell rings I immediately go outside, hop on my bus, then sit in my usual seat behind the driver. I glance out the window to see Ashlynn, Paisley, and Lexi standing together in our usual spot, looking around as if they're wondering where I am. I don't care, though. I just need time by myself to think without their incessant jabber about things that don't matter.

I don't get a ton of time to think, though, as the ride home is only about ten minutes. I step off the bus and hear Preston do the same a second later. The bus pulls away and we go our separate ways without a word. I begin my ascent up the hill toward my house, and as I look up from my feet, I see a small moving truck in our driveway, packed boxes littering the space around it. We're not supposed to be moving for another three weeks. Why is there a moving truck here already?

I quicken my pace, feeling suddenly like I'm about to cry because I've never had so many confusing things happen to me in a 24-hour period. I walk through the open garage into the house, ready to unleash the wrath hidden under all of my confusion onto my mom, who had better explain to me what has been going on and why she and Dad lied to me about him losing his job. But then I see her pink-tinged face – sweat pouring down her forehead – as she sits on the floor and carefully but quickly wraps some of her vinyl records in bubble wrap and places them in a small box. It's hard to tell since she's already wet with sweat, but it looks like she has been crying recently.

"Mom?" I ask tentatively, purposely keeping my distance. Seeing others upset makes me really uncomfortable.

She looks up, startled at seeing me standing there, watching her.

"Oh, hey Janey girl," she begins as she wipes her face with her sleeve, looking back down at the task at hand. "Uh, your father and I need to talk to you. I don't want you to ask any questions yet, though. Not until we can . . . explain better," she stammered. "Go put your stuff in your room and come down to the living room. Dad's already home."

My confusion, and now concern, are building even more.

"But wait, what's –"

"Jane. I said no questions yet. Do as I say," Mom says curtly, not bothering to even look at me.

Taken aback by her tone, I turn to the stairs and slowly make my way up, glancing back at her to see she's already resumed placing more records in the box. I swivel my head, looking at my feet as they climb the carpeted stairs, tears welling up in my eyes. Mom never speaks to me that way. She's always so gentle, kind, and predictable.

I blink away the tears, toss my backpack in my room, and step into the bathroom to look in the mirror to make sure there's no trace of hurt or bewilderment left on my face. I don't want to give Mom and Dad any reason to have to worry about me, as it's clear they have plenty more things to worry about…and I only know about one of them.

I get to the living room, briefly wondering where Scout is, but then remember that it's Wednesday and she's having her weekly playdate with a little boy down the street. I sit on the edge of the couch and wait semi-patiently. A few minutes later, Mom and Dad walk in with pleasant looks on their faces. Mom's face is so different than it was just ten minutes ago that I'm stunned into silence. Dad speaks first.

"So, honey, I'm sure you're wondering why there's a moving van here, and why I'm home early," he says.

I know why you're home early. But you decided to keep that from me for a whole day.

"I know you have a lot of questions, Jane, but I want you to wait until I'm done speaking, okay?" I nod, and he continues.

"Yesterday, my boss called me into his office and told me that my job at the museum is no longer needed. So, as of right now, I don't have a job." He pauses, as if waiting for my reaction, but I just sit there, staring. He glances at Mom, then keeps going. "Because of this, it makes more sense for us to move out of this house quicker and go somewhere…else."

"Okay . . . the new house, right?" I interrupt, wondering why he's being so evasive about something I already knew was happening.

Then, it occurs to me that the moving truck outside is not nearly big enough to hold all of our stuff. I'm suddenly worried that we're going to have to move to a house with less than four bedrooms and then there won't be a media room. Or worse, Scout and I will have to share a *bedroom* as well as a bathroom. I can't believe it..

"Well . . . not exactly," Dad answers, "since, uh, I won't have a job for a while, we need to save money, so we, um…" He trails off, obviously struggling to answer my simple question.

"What is it? You can tell me. I can handle it," I reassure him.

After another glance at Mom, he seems to decide something then finally spits it out.

"On Friday, we're going to leave this house and live with Nana for a while. She has graciously offered to put us up until I can find a job. We, uh, didn't want to buy a house until we, um… knew where I was going to be working. That way, we can for sure live somewhere that is close to my new job."

Wait, what? This doesn't make any sense.

"Okay . . ." I pause, trying to figure out how to introduce my questions calmly and carefully, without causing the crease between Dad's worried eyes to become any deeper. "Why do we have to move so fast? I didn't think we were actually moving for a few more weeks? And isn't Nana's house super small? Where is all of our stuff gonna go? How long will we be there?" So much for being calm. Once my questions started spilling out, I couldn't stop them.

Dad looks like he would rather be anywhere else than having this conversation with me. Mom must notice, too, because she speaks up.

"Jane, there are some things you just can't understand… yet. We're moving so fast because that's what your father and I decided was best. Yes, your Nana's house is pretty small, but we're just going to have to make it work because that's what we need to do right now while Dad looks for a job. A lot of our things are going to go into a storage unit for now, and we're only going to bring suitcases with essentials to Nana's house.

"As for how long we're going to be there, it shouldn't be for very long. Like we said, it's only until Dad finds a job, and then we can find a place that's close to it. That makes sense, doesn't it?" she asks, a bit patronizingly.

I nod, but it's a partial lie. It *does* make sense that they would want to wait to buy a new house until Dad gets a new job. I get that. But, what I *don't* get is why Nana's house? Couldn't we just move into a nice apartment until they figure everything out? My heart is starting to beat quicker than it should and I feel a lump start to form in my throat like it always does when I start to get upset. I take a deep breath and decide that it is probably best to just play along like this is completely normal. There's something troubling about Dad's defeated expression, the uncharacteristic fire behind Mom's eyes, and the fact that neither of them has explained why Mr. Perry coming over yesterday made them start to act so strange.

I give both of them a slight smile, then say, "Well, it'll be good to spend some time with Nana. She lives so close but we hardly ever get to see her anymore. I'll start packing up my room. Let me know what else I can do to help."

My quick change of demeanor catches them by surprise, but they seem to decide not to acknowledge it. They simply encourage me that packing would be great and then send me on my way. So I do, feeling completely in the dark as the sun shines bright through my bedroom window.

3

I have to take a different bus home today. Well, not home. It's finally Friday, and the shock of everything that happened on Wednesday has worn off considerably. But that's probably because we've been so busy the past two days. I didn't realize just how many things I owned until I had to pack it all away within thirty-six hours.

Mom and Dad have been rather frantic, working tirelessly to get everything packed away into boxes and stuffed into the moving van or taken to the new storage unit. Mom wanted me to bring my suitcase to school today then take it to Nana's with me on the bus, since there's not a lot of room in the car right now. But I begged her not to make me . . . I haven't told *anyone*, not even Ashlynn, about what's been going on. All my friends already knew that I was moving but I never told them where, and now they really don't get to know . . . it's too embarrassing.

I say a private goodbye to our house as I leave to walk to the bus, knowing I will never return to live in this glorious place ever again. My heart hurts. I don't think my parents really understand how much this is affecting me. This house is our *home*. Scout and I both grew up here. Our height marks are notched into a post in the gazebo. Our handprints are imprinted into the concrete of our back patio that was poured a few years ago. It was a Christmas gift from Mr. Perry, who owns (in addition to a lot of other businesses) a local construction company. Now, all of a sudden, I'm expected to be perfectly fine with leaving – bringing only a single suitcase with me to my great-grandmother's house.

We haven't spent a ton of time with Nana over the last few years. She's my dad's grandmother, on his mom's side. When I was little, and my PawPaw was still alive, I would go over to their house all the time. We would play board games, she would cook me spaghetti, and then we'd always have stovetop popcorn while we watched a movie on her vintage, clunky VCR. Some people might not think that sounds like fun, but it is… was. When PawPaw died just a few weeks after Scout was born, we stopped visiting. I guess we all just got busy after that and didn't have much time to spend together. Now that I think about it, it's kind of surprising that Nana's letting us stay with her since we've made very little effort to see her over the last four years. I mean, Scout barely knows her.

Though thankfully, Scout can make friends with anyone and she's actually been immensely excited to stay at Nana's. She's so oblivious to everything that happens in this family. It's all sunshine and daisies in that one's eyes. Must be nice.

The bus finally arrives, and I notice that Preston is nowhere to be found. I look across the street to the Oakwood apartments just in case he's on his way over, then I can tell the driver to wait for him.

But I don't see him – just a stray dog running around looking for scraps. Preston must have overslept. Hopefully his mom can bring him to school because we have presentations due today in English class. I start to wonder if he's okay when I remember that I don't care. If Lexi is going to have a crush on Preston then it's better if I distance myself, even my thoughts, from him. That way, Lexi and Paisley and even Ashlynn have no reason to think that I'm interested in him. Heaven forbid anyone else has the same thoughts or feelings as they do.

I get to school and the day is much the same as any other day. I get off the bus, listen to my friends gossip about this, that, and the other; I go to class, do my work; next class, more work, on and on and on. But by my last class of the day, I begin to feel more and more uneasy about the simple task of getting on a bus. My friends will definitely notice when I walk on a bus that is definitely *not* going in the direction of where our new house was supposed to be. What will they say? What will *I* say?

As Mrs. Gentry drones on about the riveting subject of quadratic equations, I attempt to devise a plan. Instead of meeting everyone by Paisley's locker before going to the commons, I'm just going to head straight there and get on the bus before anyone sees. That will work. Then I'll have the whole weekend to come up with the reason why I didn't stop by her locker. I'm such a genius - they won't suspect a thing.

My plan works flawlessly. I speed walk to my new bus and sit on the side that faces the street so no one spots me through the window. Thankfully, there's not a lot of people that ride this bus, so I'm not too at risk of being noticed by anyone important. Not that I know any of them anyway. They're not quite the type of people I would choose to be around. As they board the bus, I recognize the faces of the kids who are always in trouble for something – skipping class, fighting, throwing food at lunch. I guess they all live in the same neighborhood . . . *my new neighborhood.*

I get off the bus at my stop along with four others, who briefly stare at me like they know I don't belong here with them. However, they don't say anything, and we go our separate ways. Nana's neighborhood sits right in the middle of town, filled with the oldest houses I've ever seen. I never got a good look at them when I was younger. I suppose I had no reason to. But now, as I walk down the long street to Nana's house – which sits at the very end of the lane – I take note of several things. Every house is only one story, there are broken down cars sitting abandoned in unkempt lawns, every street sign is lopsided, and some houses have solid iron bars over their windows. I walk faster.

Approaching Nana's house, it's clear she takes much better care of her house and yard than everyone else in the neighborhood. Her house is quaint – with bird feeders, wind chimes, and flower beds galore. I unlatch the short, picket-fence gate and walk up the lane toward the house, securing the latch behind me. Our moving van is sitting in front of the carport, boxing in Nana's clunky old car. That's okay, though. She doesn't drive anymore since PawPaw died. Dad says she gets help from a local organization who sends people over to help her with cooking, cleaning, taking her to doctor's appointments, or the grocery store, things like that. Yesterday we came over for just a minute to drop off a few things, and I saw one of their cars in the driveway. I didn't go inside, though. Dad had told Scout and I to wait in the car.

But now, I have no choice but to go inside, or else risk being recognized and subsequently ridiculed by someone from school who actually knows who I am. I push open the faded green front door and enter directly into the living room. There's no foyer here. Scout, who had been playing with her dolls on the stained carpeted floor, hops up when she sees me and puts her skinny little arms around my middle. I can't help but grin. Sure, she's the most annoying human on the planet, but she's the only one who's always excited to see me.

Nana is sitting in her recliner, watching us with a small smile. I haven't seen her in years. I detach myself from Scout and cross the room to greet Nana, bending down to give her a hug.

"Hey, there, Snugglebug," she says as we embrace, patting me gently on the back. "It's so nice to finally see you again. You've grown so much!"

"You, too," I reply. "Your house is really . . . nice," I say hesitantly as I look around the space. The low-hanging ceiling, dim lighting, and musty smell gives the impression of a flea market that is in desperate need of an upgrade.

I quickly take a glance down the hallway that branches off from the living room, and see four closed doors that I assume lead to the bedrooms and bathrooms. The kitchen sits directly behind Nana, and it looks like something straight out of my history book about the 1970s. There are old appliances, a counter that has big chips taken out of it on some of the edges, and instead of a dishwasher there's a washing machine with no dryer. Though one quick look at the layer of dust that has settled on it tells me the thing hasn't worked in years. The house looked so much better from the outside. Guess I shouldn't have judged a book by its cover.

I look back down at Nana, and see her watching my face carefully. She looks like she wants to say something, but then must think better of it, because she just invites me to put my backpack down and have a seat on the cracked faux leather couch.

"Where are Mom and Dad?" I ask her.

"Oh, they're out organizing your new storage unit. They should be back soon," she replies.

I nod, feeling quite awkward in the silence that follows.

"Would it be okay if I turned on the TV?" I ask, not willing to tolerate the painful quiet any longer.

"Oh, sweetheart, I haven't had a television in so long. Cable just got too expensive, and I've found much better ways to occupy my time," says Nana.

My mouth involuntarily hangs open as I hear her reply. *No TV?!* That's crazy! What does she *do* all day? The absurdity of not owning a TV in the twenty-first century would be enough to keep me puzzled for days, but then another part of her response sticks out to me. She said cable was *too expensive.* I've seen ads for cable hookup. You can get it for only fifty bucks a month! That's barely anything. I would guess that the *real* reason she doesn't have one is because she's old school and refuses to adjust to the times, because *everyone* can afford fifty dollars a month for TV. Our TV is in the moving van. I'm sure my parents will hook it up when they get back, then pay for us to have cable for however long we're staying here. Yes, that will be good. Then we can show Nana the joys of Tuesday night Jeopardy.

I feel better after thinking this through, and decide to play with Scout and her dolls. Scout is beside herself with excitement that I decided to do so. It seems like all this moving and change has had no effect whatsoever on her life. When my parents told her we were moving in with Nana, she ran to her room with a huge smile on her face and began to throw things into her tiny, purple, glittery suitcase. Good for her. She doesn't have to think about how all of this reflects on her social status at school.

Mom and Dad get home about an hour later, though it feels like it should be tomorrow by now. The clock on the wall seems to be moving in slow motion. As they walk through the front door, I stand up, stretching my sore back. I'm not used to sitting on the floor with Scout for so long, but I had nothing else to occupy my time. As we played, Nana sat quietly in her recliner, doing a crossword puzzle from one of those cheap books you can get at the dollar store. How is *that* better than TV? I'm still baffled by the idea.

Mom cooks spaghetti for dinner, but it's made with plain canned spaghetti sauce with no beef. The mushy green beans are also from a can, and the garlic bread is just white sandwich bread that she put in the toaster and topped with butter and garlic powder. I involuntarily and unknowingly make a face when it is served. I mean, I know Dad doesn't have a job right now, but why are we eating like poor people? This is the type of food we served that one time at our old church for the *homeless* people.

"Jane, what's with the face?" Mom asks, setting a pitcher of ice water on the table.

I look up at her, finding it difficult to actually correct my expression.

"I don't mean to complain," I start, "but I thought we'd be having pizza tonight, since it's Friday." Ok, that sort of works. We've had pizza on several Fridays before.

"Nope, no pizza," Mom says as she settles into her chair, placing a thin paper towel in her lap. "This is what I decided to make, so that's what we're having. A 'thank you' would be nice, since I took the time to actually prepare this meal for everyone."

I can tell that I said the wrong thing. I shouldn't have said anything at all. I don't like being reprimanded by anyone, but especially my parents. I wasn't *trying* to be ungrateful or complain, but how can they expect me to just be *okay* with eating this?! I hope that this is just because they didn't have a chance to go to the store yet, and this was what Nana had in her pantry.

I say a small "thank you" to her, but don't say anything else for the rest of the meal. Mom seems so on edge this week. This has been hard for *all* of us. Why does *she* get to be all snippy when I was just asking a simple question? We eat in near silence. No one says their highs, lows, or buffalos.

After dinner, there's not much to do except play with Scout some more, so that's what I do while Mom and Dad have yet another long, private conversation somewhere else in the house. I can't try and eavesdrop right now, though. Not with Nana sitting so close.

When it's nearing bedtime, I ask Nana which room I'm staying in. Before she can answer, Dad cuts in, saying he'll show me to the room. He leads me down the short hallway and opens the first door on the left. I walk in to see a queen-sized bed, air mattresses on either side of it. All four of our suitcases are piled in one corner, and a tall, dim lamp stands in the other, doing very little to brighten the space.

I begin to put the pieces together, and realize that my parents intend for all of us to sleep in the same room. My parents in the bed, and Scout and I each on one of the sagging air mattresses. I'm thunderstruck. And even though Mom is in a foul mood, I feel it's safe to talk to Dad about all this.

"Dad, do we *really* all have to sleep in this *one* room? What about the other rooms?" I ask him, trying to keep my voice sounding pleasantly inquisitive.

"Well, this is a two-bedroom house. Nana has her room, and this is the guest room. Then there's one bathroom for all five of us to share. I know it's not ideal, but this is what we have to work with for the time being. Nana has been really kind to let us stay with her while we get this figured out. It's only going to be for a little while, remember? I'm going to start looking for a new job this weekend, then we can move somewhere else," he says.

Now that I'm thinking about it, I don't know why I assumed that I would have my own bedroom at Nana's — of course there aren't that many rooms. But, the rest of what he said is the same thing they've been telling us all week. That he will get a new job, we'll move to a place that's close to it, and everything will go back to normal. I want to believe that, but it's really difficult when everything is as far from normal as it could possibly get.

4

I don't sleep well. The air mattress must have a tiny leak in it somewhere, because I wake up around three o'clock and I'm nearly touching the floor. I can't air it back up now, though, because my parents and Scout are sleeping only inches away. So I just lie there for a few hours, uncomfortable, hot, and nearly going deaf as Dad's train-like snores rattle the thin glass on the window.

As seven o'clock rolls around, my family finally starts to stir, and I get up acting like I had the best sleep of my life. I don't want Mom to jump on my case again for being ungrateful or for complaining, even though I have plenty of reason and justification to do so. I just think I need to be more careful around her until we're settled in wherever we end up living next. Her usual calm, sweet, and kind personality has been difficult to find over these past few days. I know all of this has been stressful for her, but it's been stressful for all of us . . . well, maybe not for Scout. She's currently bouncing on her knees on top of the pilled bedspread, lost in her own world.

We each have an instant oatmeal packet for breakfast, with a glass of milk to help wash it down. On a normal weekend, I would go over to one of my friend's houses, or they would come to mine since we all live – lived – in the same neighborhood. Now, I'm not sure what I'm going to do to keep busy. I'm thinking I could maybe take a walk around Nana's neighborhood, but then I remember how uncomfortable I felt just walking down the street from the bus stop yesterday. It's definitely not safe to do that here, even in the daylight.

I'm still trying to figure out how to spend my day when Dad tells me he needs me to stay here and watch Scout while he and Mom go out and try to find him a new job. This seems unfair. She's not *my* kid.

"Why can't Nana watch Scout, and I come with you guys?" I ask.

"Jane, stop with the backtalk. I'm sick of it!" Mom suddenly exclaims.

"I wasn't trying to–," I try to defend myself.

"No. Nana needs rest, and we're probably going to be gone the whole day. Just do what we ask the first time. What is so hard about that? You're going to stay here and take care of Scout. Be respectful to your Nana, and don't go wandering around the neighborhood. There's a couple of cans of ravioli in the pantry that you can microwave for lunch. We'll be back around dinnertime." She doesn't even bother to look at me.

I stand there, shell-shocked, staring at her back as she walks out the front door. Dad gives me a sad smile, pats me gently on the shoulder, then follows her out.

I hear a pair of tiny feet pitter patter to me, then pause.

"Jane? What's wrong? Are you crying?" Scout asks me tentatively, holding two of my fingers in her petite hand.

I look down and see her face. It's obvious she's worried about me, but the semi-vacant look in her eyes reminds me that she really doesn't have any clue what's going on. I know I shouldn't, since she's so little and can't help it, but I resent her in this moment. No one would ever *dare* yell at the baby. They'd never make *her* babysit all day on a Saturday, never *ever* make *her* feel like a selfish brat. Why should I be nice to her when no one is being nice to me?

Lost in the heat of my anger, I yank my hand out of her grasp.

"Of course I'm not crying. Go find something to do and leave me alone." I hear her sniffle as she goes back to the bedroom. I don't feel bad, though. It's about time she feels some emotion other than unrequited happiness.

I sit down on the couch and close my eyes, hoping that I can catch up on a little bit of sleep. A few minutes later, Nana hobbles into the living room. I slightly open my eyes, and notice that she sits down in her recliner, picks up her crossword book and a dull pencil, and begins to work on a puzzle, just as she did last night. I shut my eyes again, hoping that she won't bother me when she sees I'm trying to rest.

"It's strange," Nana says. "A few minutes ago, I thought I heard crying coming from the bedroom. Any idea why that might be?"

I raise my head and look at her. She's still looking down at her crossword puzzle, waiting for my response.

"Uh, yeah…" I begin, sitting up. "Scout was just being sensitive. She asked about her princess pony show, and I told her there wasn't a TV so she couldn't watch it. Then she got really upset," I lie. I don't want Nana to think that I intentionally hurt Scout's feelings, even though I very much did.

Nana's now looking at me over her crossword, her eyes piercing me over the short stretch of space between us. I instantly feel ashamed. I get that feeling I used to always get as a kid when I was with her – the feeling that she was reading my mind as if it were a large-print open book. Nana was such an important person in my life before Scout was born – before PawPaw died. Even though I haven't spent hardly any time with her since, I can tell she thinks she still knows me. But she doesn't. I'm a completely different person now than I was when I was ten. And she doesn't know Scout at all. I can't believe she's accusing me of being hurtful to Scout. *Oh, wait.* I was. But she hasn't said a word in response to my lie. She just nods and resumes her crossword in silence, as if what I said made perfect sense.

No longer wanting to be subjected to my own guilt floating in the stuffy air of the living room, I get up from the couch and walk outside to the front porch, abandoning my hopes of getting in a couch-nap. When I close the front door behind me, I'm expecting fresh air, but instead I'm pelted by the distinctive stench of cigarettes from one of Nana's neighbors, who I see smoking in a cheap folding chair on her own front porch. Even from here, I can see the fatigue in her eyes, the disheveled look of her overall appearance, and the very obvious aura that she is not very friendly. She notices me when I walk out, but quickly looks away, minding her own business. Good.

I sit down on the front step, not knowing what to do next. I know I'm not supposed to walk around the neighborhood, but there's really not much else to do. I seriously contemplate taking a lap around the neighborhood's loop anyway, but ultimately decide against it. I don't want to get in any more trouble right now, especially since I'm not entirely sure what I did wrong this morning to warrant the verbal onslaught by my mother.

I eventually settle on watching a small, bright yellow bird perched on the edge of one of the feeders in the lawn. It makes quite the mess, flinging the sunflower seed shells all around the grass. Then it flutters away, surely landing somewhere amongst the branches of the large oak tree that stands tall between Nana's house and her neighbors'. I wish I were that bird. Free to do whatever I want; go wherever I want . . . peaceful.

I don't know how long I sit on the porch, but I'm brought back to the present by the sound of gravel crunching in the driveway. I look up to see a rusted, red pickup truck pulling into Nana's house. It looks vaguely familiar, but I can't quite place it . . . and I can't see who's sitting inside due to the glare on the windshield from the sun. Since I don't know who this could be, I get up from my step to go inside and let Nana know that someone's here. But before I can, the doors to the truck open and my stomach gives a nervous lurch. I see his scuffed-up sneakers first, then move my gaze up to see him flick his bangs out of his face. It's Preston Miller.

I go into panic mode. I'm frozen on the outside, but inside I'm on fire. *What is he doing here?* There's someone with him. Is that his mom? It probably is . . . I think I've seen her before. What is *she* doing here? What are *either* of them doing here?

My hands are clammy, and I'm feeling frantic. They're going to figure out that we're living here. Then they'll know that we had to move and that Dad lost his job and that we're basically living like poor people right now. But before I can run, hide, or both, Preston sees me standing on the porch. His face looks bewildered, his eyebrows raised in surprise. He quickly glances from me to his mom then to the house behind me. He didn't expect to see me here, which means he probably doesn't know what has happened to me – us.

Preston's mom looks at me too, then looks at her son, seeing the confusion and concern on his face. I can tell she knows that he recognizes me, or she herself knows who I am from seeing me at the bus stop or at school functions. She turns back toward me, a friendly smile appearing on her face as she cuts across the lawn to reach the porch. Preston trails several steps behind her, holding a mop bucket filled with cleaning supplies.

"Hi!" Preston's mom says brightly. "I'm Mrs. Miller, Preston's mom," she says, gesturing for him to come closer. "You know Preston from school, right? Don't you two ride the same bus?"

I decide to use the question as an opportunity to fabricate my cover-up story.

"Yeah, we ride the same bus… I see Preston almost every morning! I'm just here, uh, visiting my great-grandmother," I say in the friendliest way I can, attempting to match Mrs. Miller's energy. "She and I are really close, so I like coming over to spend time with her. In fact, she and I were just about to sit down together. She wants to teach me how to do crossword puzzles," I continue, thinking that it's good to really sell it for all it's worth.

"Oh, that's wonderful!" Mrs. Miller replies. "Well then she must have told you about us, then! We'll just go ahead and get started," she says as she walks past me to open the front door and enter the house. "We've got a few stops today, so there's no time to waste!"

I'm left on the porch with Preston, who looks at me just as I am looking at him, though I'm sure feeling vastly different things. *I* am feeling a concoction of emotions that includes confusion as to why Preston and his mother are at my Nana's house, mixed with a sensation close to fear that they will figure out the real reason I'm here. If I had to guess, though I hope I'm wrong, what I see behind Preston's creased eyebrows is complete doubt that my story holds any ounce of truth. However, he just gives me a slight nod, then follows his mom into the house.

Determined to get to the bottom of this strange turn of events, I follow them. Mrs. Miller is bending down to give Nana a hug in greeting. Nana's face is lit up with a grin, showing much more delight in seeing the Millers than she has with any of us over the last day of my family being here.

"Oh, have you met my great-granddaughter? This is Jane," Nana says, gesturing to me. "Her family is–"

"– just visiting for the weekend! It's been so nice to see my Nana so far," I interrupt quickly, before she can reveal my secret to these people who she obviously thinks are much more exciting to see than her own family.

Nana searches me in an instant, then smiles and nods once, looking back at Mrs. Miller and Preston.

"Yes well, Preston, dear," Nana addresses him (who had been giving me a reproachful look), "I would appreciate it so much if you could work on the lawn today. That would really help me out. And Penny, I would be ever so grateful if you could tackle the dishes. The mess from supper last night is all still in the sink. Jane, you need to go check on Scout and see if she is alright."

"Of course, Mrs. McCarthy," Preston replies with a pleasant expression, as if there's nothing he'd rather be doing than mowing Nana's scruffy yard. He hands the bucket of cleaning supplies to his mom, then heads out into the backyard toward the squat shed that houses the lawnmower. He doesn't even bother to give me a backward glance.

"It's nice to meet you, Jane," Mrs. Miller says. As she walks toward the kitchen, I see her take a glance out the back window toward her son, then back at me, before she turns the corner to get started on the dishes. The sound of water filling the sink drowns out Nana's next comments.

"You know, Jane, I think you're going to be here longer than just the weekend. It may make more sense not to hide that fact from people, especially your friends," she says.

"Preston is *not* my friend," I say quickly.

"Did I say he was?" Nana replies.

Frustrated and even more confused, I decide to quickly check on Scout in the bedroom, who I see has fallen asleep on the bed. I guess she didn't sleep well last night, either. I then walk outside to confront Preston about what in the world he is doing at my Nana's house, because there's not a lot of room for coincidence in our town, seeing as how there's so many people. Hopefully I can further convince him that I, we, do not, under any circumstances, actually *live* here.

As I walk across the grassy lawn, ankles tickled from the tall vegetation, I can see Preston walking backwards as he drags the old push-mower out of the shed. As he gives one final pull so the mower falls into the grass, he wheels it around and looks up to see me standing there.

"Oh hey, Princess," Preston says. My eyes instinctively roll to the back of my head. I'm so sick of that nickname. It's not funny anymore.

"Stop calling me Princess! It's annoying," I demand.

Preston smirks as he squats to prime the engine of the mower.

"I don't know . . . I think the name fits you perfectly," he says.

"How do you suppose?" I ask, interested to hear just what he thinks warrants the patronizing name.

"Well, let's see. You live in ValleyRidge, so you basically reside in a castle as your house. You get everything you want, nothing you own is from a thrift store, and it seems as though everyone at school wants to be you," he rattles off, still focusing on the mower.

My mouth opens to respond, but my reply gets stuck in my chest. Do people really want to *be* me? I have never been given that impression. I've heard that about Paisley or Lexi, sure, but not me.

"No one has any reason to want to be me," I say as I cross my arms, suddenly feeling insecure.

"And why do you say that?" he asks, still fiddling around with the lawnmower.

Plenty of reasons, I think. My dad has no job. I'm living in one room, with my entire family, in my great-grandmother's house which is in the oldest and sketchiest part of town. I'm having to eat food from a can. My little sister is as annoying as ever. My mom seems like she is finding any and all reasons to yell at me. And *now* I'm standing in an overgrown backyard defending myself to my least favorite classmate. But, of course, I can't say any of this to Preston, so I decide to be vague.

"There's just a lot going on in people's lives that other people don't know. So they shouldn't judge," I say.

Preston finishes whatever he's doing with the mower and stands back up, a small sheen of sweat dampening his long bangs.

"That's very true. So why do you judge other people so much, then?" he retorts.

"What do you mean? I don't judge people for anything," I say quite unconfidently, suddenly feeling more insecure than ever.

"Yeah, okay," he says, grinning slightly again, "but just so you know, even if people can't read your mind, they can still read your face."

What does that mean — 'read my face'? I'm starting to get extremely annoyed with this conversation, but then remember why I came out here in the first place.

"Why are you here? How do you know my Nana?" I ask.

Preston rubs the back of his neck.

"My mom and I volunteer with an organization that helps elderly people with things they're not able to do anymore, or just things they need to get done. Mrs. McCarthy is one of our regulars, so we come here every Saturday and help her out," he explains.

"Oh…" I say, feeling inferior. "How long have you been volunteering?"

"For a couple of years now, since I was in sixth grade," he answers. "And it's funny . . . Mrs. McCarthy has never *ever* told me about her family visiting her. You'd think, since you come over so often, that she would have said something about you. Weird, isn't it?"

Uh-oh. Busted. I think quickly, trying to come up with something to explain this inconsistency between my lies and the truth.

"Well, actually, her memory is fading fast. You know, that happens to people when they get to be really old. She probably just forgot."

I pause, trying to read Preston's face as easily as he said people can read mine. But his face seems blank. No, not blank – thinking. He's looking at me with his piercing green eyes that are obviously judging me, but that are also, surprisingly, kind. I abruptly get the feeling that if I come clean about what's been going on, he won't tell anyone anything. He'll keep my secrets. But then I'm reminded about what he really thinks of me – that I'm an entitled, spoiled brat. He would take the first chance he could to ruin me if he was presented with the opportunity.

Preston doesn't respond to my comment about Nana's memory, which in reality is perfectly intact. He starts the mower, which idles loudly and spews out nasty fumes identical to those at a go-kart track.

"I SHOULD PROBABLY GET GOING ON THIS!" Preston shouts over the rumble of the engine.

I give him a thumbs up, my mouth tightened into a thin line that I'm hoping looks like a soft smile, and return to the house.

I give a brief "hello" to Prestons' mom as I pass her in the kitchen and head to the bedroom, feeling like I could definitely use a nap now. I gently lie next to Scout's sleeping figure. I try to dissect my conversation with Preston while becoming increasingly paranoid about the fact that he saw me here, and that he probably knows Nana so much better than even I do. Though his assessment of who I am as a person rattles me most of all — especially that piece about how others view me.

My eyes quickly become heavy as the stress of the past twenty-four hours overtake me, and I drift off to a restless sleep.

5

It's Monday, the day I had been dreading all weekend. By the time I had woken up from my mid-morning nap on Saturday, Preston and Mrs. Miller had gone. In the afternoon, I watched Scout play in the freshly cut backyard while I read a rather boring book for school. That night at dinner, which consisted of Spanish rice and refried beans with tortillas, I dared to ask if Dad had found a job while they were out that day. He said he hadn't, but didn't elaborate.

At this point, I'm not even sure where he's applying or what type of job he's trying to get. I know that the jobs he's qualified for — academic-type things — are sure to be rather sparse around here. We don't have any colleges or universities. There's only one small private school that I doubt is hiring, and the only museum in town decided that Dad was no longer of value to be employed there. I wonder how long it's going to take for him to get a job… a week? Two? How long will we have to live with Nana? Because I'm sure that as long as he's not working, we're not going anywhere anytime soon. The prospect fills me with dread.

Another thought filling me with dread is the idea of seeing Preston at school today. As the weekend went on, I convinced myself that he absolutely did not buy my story that we were just visiting Nana. For one, our moving van was sitting right there in the driveway. If he's been over there every week for the last two years, he definitely noticed that anomaly. Pair that with him spotlighting that Nana has never mentioned us visiting her, and it's clear to anyone that I made it all up.

It's a foggy, chilly morning as I stand at the end of the street, waiting for the bus to pick me and several others up for school. I can hear some of them chatting behind me as I lean sideways against the stop sign, feeling alone . . . again. I'm also unbelievably exhausted. Each night has been worse than the last, all of us trying to sleep in one room. I just hope that the bags under my eyes don't show too bad. But I'm sure they will, seeing as I only got about four decent hours of sleep last night.

As we ride to school, a realization hits me out of nowhere. I didn't come up with what I'm going to tell Ashlynn, Lexi, and Paisley about why I didn't meet them at the lockers Friday afternoon! And when we get to school, they're going to see me get off of this bus! Then they'll know that I'm not living where we were supposed to be living. They'll see the type of people that ride this bus, and inevitably put two and two together about which neighborhood I came from. Only a few blocks left – quick – what am I going to say?!

I sort through my options. Maybe I could just play it cool – act like nothing's wrong – but then they're bound to ask me a million questions. Come clean and tell them everything that's happened over the last week? No, it's too horrifying; they'd never understand. And then there's the chance they'd spread rumors that would go out of control fast. Avoid them? That may work – I'd get some more time to come up with an excuse. I decide to take that route as I get off the bus and step into the courtyard. I'm frantically searching for a path of escape. Perhaps I could make it inside before they see me. We're allowed to go inside early if we want to go to the library or to breakfast. But I'm not fast enough.

"Jane!" a familiar voice shouts behind me.

I cringe, beating myself up inside that I didn't think about this plan sooner. I turn to see Ashlynn walking toward me across the lawn. Behind her, Lexi and Paisley stay where they are in their usual spot, whispering to each other as they stare in our direction. It's pretty clear who they're talking about. As Ashlynn approaches, I can see her awkward-looking face, as if she doesn't know how to act separated from the group. Her arms are crossed over her chest, and she's looking at me like I'm a wounded animal she'd rather not approach. Since escape is out of the question, I decide to go with option number one.

"Hey!" I return her greeting. "I was just going to go to the library to finish some homework that I didn't get to this weekend. Want to come?"

Okay, this is suspicious enough because I always finish all my homework. And not once in our nearly three years of middle school have I *ever* wanted to go to the library in the morning. But it's the only thing that explains why I didn't immediately join the three of them in our usual spot. And if she accuses me of anything, I could treat her like *she's* the one acting odd, because I'm well within my rights as a student to go to the library.

Ashlynn's standing there facing me, but she's finding it difficult to meet my eyes. Her arms are still crossed, and she's looking around as if to make sure she's not being overheard.

"Yeah, um, I… or, we… the three of us… wanted to talk to you about something," she says nervously.

"If the three of you wanted to talk to me, then why are Lexi and Paisley standing over there?" I ask, pointing at the other two, not bothering to hide it.

Ashlynn glances over her shoulder at them, then continues, more embarrassed sounding than ever.

"Um, well they wanted me to bring it up to you first, since you and I are so close."

I wait, wondering what she knows, how she knows it, and where this conversation is going. Secondary to those questions, though, I wonder what her definition of 'close' is because I feel so disconnected from all three of them right now.

"You know how Paisley's mom and Preston Miller's mom both go to the same church?" Ashlynn asks me.

I actually didn't know that, but I just nod along like I did.

"Well, on Sunday, they were talking at church. And I guess Preston's mom told Paisley's mom that she met you at one of the old lady's houses that they visit to help out. And…" she pauses, glancing again at Lexi and Paisley, who are watching us with smug looks on their faces. "And . . . I guess she said you went and *talked* to Preston while he was there."

Sweet relief washes over me. *This* I can explain away.

"Oh, yeah!" I say brightly, as if this is the most normal thing I've ever talked about. "My family was visiting my Nana for the weekend. You know her – she's my dad's grandma – I've talked about her before. While we were there, Preston and his mom showed up to help Nana out. I had NO idea they had been doing that every week! Isn't that really nice of them?" I briefly pause, trying to gauge Ashlynn's reception of this information, when I instantly recall the last sentence she said. I wait to see what she says first before addressing it.

"Oh, yeah…" she begins, waving her hand at me indifferently. "That's what we figured." I don't think she was expecting me to respond in such a positive, nonchalant way. She continues, "Uh, well, Paisley's mom told Paisley, who told Lexi, that you had gone and *talked to Preston* while he was over there."

I shake my head and slightly shrug my shoulders.

"Okay? Is there something wrong with that?" I ask, intending to provoke her into telling me what she, or Lexi, for that matter, truly think about that. Though I'm sure I already know the answer.

Ashlynn looks like she'd rather be anywhere else, but the peer pressure of the two girls standing watching is getting to be too much for her. She closes her eyes, then opens them, looking straight into mine, seeming to gather her courage.

"Well, Lexi is super upset because you were talking to him just a few days after she told you that she liked him. She thinks you're trying to take him from her before she's even gotten the chance to talk to him herself. And she also wanted me to tell you that she's not going to talk to you until you apologize for doing that. And you have to promise never to talk to him again."

Ashlynn finally has the decency to drop her gaze. I am dumbfounded. Angry. I knew Lexi was shallow – that all of them were – but I didn't expect *this* to be what they were so worried about. She hasn't brought up the bus, or why I didn't meet them at the lockers, or even my disheveled appearance that I know I have from trying to get ready in the tiniest bathroom in the world. None of it.

I can't help but laugh a little bit, which takes Ashlynn aback. I lean to my right to look directly at Lexi and Paisley as I pretend to be addressing Ashlynn. My voice raises so they can hear me across the courtyard.

"Ok, well if she's worried about me 'stealing him', you can tell her that that is not going to happen in a million years. Oh, and I'm not apologizing to *anyone*! If she can't buck up enough to come talk to me herself, then I'm for sure not going to be talking to her. So tell her to come find me if she wants to try that again. I don't care one bit if she doesn't talk to me as a 'punishment' for simply talking to another human being."

I turn on my heel and storm away right as the bell rings to signal the start of the day, not bothering to look back to see their reactions.

I guess that's the end of my friendship with Lexi, then. How *dare* she act like I'm not allowed to talk to whoever I want, but *especially* accuse me of trying to 'take' Preston from her. Uh, newsflash, Lexi – YOU DON'T OWN HIM! I don't even care about Preston, really. I just hate the way Lexi thinks. All *three* of them, for that matter. Paisley is such a blabbermouth. Why is she telling Lexi anything about me anyway? And Lexi having poor Ashlynn do her dirty work? And Ashlynn agreeing to it?! I am baffled.

Though, I guess I shouldn't be too hard on Ashlynn. It was clear she didn't want to be talking to me about any of it. And I'd bet the other two bullied her, like they always do, into doing what they wanted. So as I sit in first period, I decide that while I won't talk to Lexi or Paisley right now, I'll still be friends with Ashlynn – for now.

I give her a small smile across the aisle between our two desks, which sit in stereotypical rows in the beige classroom. The rest of the class files in, a couple people giving me sidelong glances, obviously having heard my shouts across the courtyard. I suddenly feel sheepish and embarrassed about my actions, but a spark of anger replaces it quickly. It's no one's business about *any* of it, and they need to mind their own. The others in the class are quite unconcerned with the happenings of my friendships, or the internal turmoil I am presently experiencing. They just sit down like nothing out of the ordinary has happened to them in the entirety of their lives. At least no one knows about what's been happening with my family . . . at least not yet.

I pull out my History notebook as the morning announcements start over the intercom. It's the same sort of messages every Monday: reminders to get your yearbook forms in, notices about clubs that I would never be caught dead being a part of, and the principal's usual spiel about refraining from intentionally clogging the toilets in the boys' bathrooms. *Ugh*. The boys at this school need to grow up.

I'm about to tune the drone out completely, when one announcement in particular catches my attention.

"We also have something very exciting coming up for our eighth-grade graduates!" intones the intercom. "Our Eighth Grade Ball will take place on May 1st, from 7pm – 9pm, here at Blossom View Middle School. Tickets will be sold by Student Council members at lunch each day until April 30th. The tickets will cost $35, which will go toward the cost of food, decorations, and the DJ. Have a marvelous Monday, Blossom View!"

The intercom cuts off with a small *pop*.

A wave of excitement courses through me. I had completely forgotten about the Eighth Grade Ball! For the past three years, all we've heard from the older students has been about how much fun it is. Everyone dresses up really nice, and there's dance music, fancy food, and door prizes!

Some people go with their boyfriends or girlfriends, but most people just go in a group, since we all know that middle school relationships don't last longer than a few months. It's better not to have your memories tainted by an immature middle school boy who can't figure out the difference between deodorant and obscene amounts of body spray. It's a good thing I've got my friends.

Oh wait. I guess I only have one friend now.

And that friend is looking at me all bright-eyed and bushy-tailed, chattering on about how excited she is for the Ball as our teacher tries to quiet the class down from the excitement of the announcement. I hope people don't think it's weird that Ashlynn and I will be going alone together, but I'm sure the rumor river has already started flowing about how Lexi and Paisley aren't my friends anymore. So everyone should understand.

But who knows? The Ball is in two weeks. There's plenty of time for them to apologize.

Our teacher finally gets the class quieted down enough by threatening lunch detention to anyone who isn't silently reading chapter twelve of their textbook. Feeling immensely more cheerful at the prospect of attending the Ball, I happily open my textbook and start reading about the Cold War, daydreaming about what color dress I will wear to this once-in-a-lifetime event.

6

I can think of little else but the Ball for the remainder of the morning. Even lunch doesn't upset me too much, as Ashlynn and I sit at an empty table on the opposite side of the cafeteria from Lexi and Paisley. Ashlynn can tell that I don't want to talk about what happened with them this morning, so the conversation turns to the Ball.

"What are you going to wear?" Ashlynn asks.

"I don't know yet, but I definitely want to get something new," I answer, "something no one's ever seen me wear before. I'm sure my mom will take me shopping this weekend to get a new dress. I think green would look really good on me, though."

"Oh yeah, for sure. I was thinking I could wear a light blue dress to bring out my eyes, and try to convince my parents to let me wear high heels. I'd have to practice walking in them, though." An idea seems to spark in Ashlynn's head. "Hey! What if I came over and we could use your mom's heels to practice walking in them before the Ball?! And then I can see your new house!"

Ashlynn's looking at me expectantly, but I'm having trouble coming up with a good excuse as to why she can't come over. The truth, that we don't even *have* a house, is not ready to be shared. But I can't afford to lose another friend today, so I need to come up with something quick.

"Actually, the house is being repainted right now," I start. "It's a big pain. When we got there to move in, there were so many chips in the wall that my parents decided it was better to just repaint the whole thing. I haven't even gotten to fully unpack yet because we can't put any of the furniture where it's supposed to go until everything is finished."

Ashlynn accepts this without a hitch.

"Oh, man, that sucks," she says. "Well, my mom probably won't even let me wear heels anyway – she has some sort of vendetta against them ever since she broke her ankle while wearing them when she was in college . . ."

Ashlynn continues talking, telling me the embarrassing story about her mom's college days. I laugh along, asking questions in all the right places, immensely relieved that she didn't ask me any follow-up questions – like what color paint we're using in the house. That would be difficult to explain away when we eventually *do* get a house again and the paint color isn't what I said it was going to be.

The bell that signals the end of lunch sounds while Ashlynn is still rambling on, telling her endless stories that have now somehow turned into one about an aunt of hers that got bit by a sea turtle in Florida. I grab my tray of uneaten chicken nuggets and soggy fries,

Ashlynn her lunchbox, and we cross the cafeteria to throw our trash away.

Since we don't have the next class together, we say goodbye and part ways. I head to Science, while Ashlynn goes to Gym. Our classes after lunch alternate each day, so today I have Science after lunch rather than before. Yeah, it's weird, but our principal thought it made sense.

When I enter the classroom, I notice a new seating chart has been posted on the whiteboard. I can hear some girls behind me complaining about it as they come in and see it for themselves. I don't mind new seating charts. I'm not like those girls that base their entire identities on their friendships, and then lose their ever-loving minds whenever they have to be apart from them for fifty-three minutes. I watch those girls as they drift apart to their new seats, their lips stuck out in a pout, reaching for each other across the space. Pathetic.

I get closer to the board to find my name and to see who my new lab partner is. I find my name in the back left corner of the classroom, then freeze instantly when I see the name written next to mine. Preston Miller.

For two years, I have managed only to be near to him during our five-minute interactions at the bus stop every morning, and now within one week, he has wormed his way into my life: at Nana's, in Lexi's brain that inevitably spilled out into words that I was forced to hear, and now as my new lab partner.

It's going to be especially difficult to keep my secrets from him, if he doesn't already know them. He seems to be very intuitive about people, like he can look at them and just know what is going on in their minds. But then I remind myself that he calls me–

"Princess Jane! Fancy seeing you here," Preston greets me, smiling as he looks up from writing in his Science notebook. He's wearing his usual selection: a stained t-shirt, tattered jeans, and disintegrating shoes. And his hair? It's scruffier than ever.

His smile is annoying. His voice is annoying. I would rather turn into a frog than be his lab partner for the last month of school.

I am silent as I set my bag on the floor, leaning it against the leg of the lab table. I get out my notebook and begin to copy down the bell ringer question, refusing to look at him.

"Oh, I see. The silent treatment again?" he asks. "Fine, be that way. I'm just trying to be nice."

"I'm not giving you the silent treatment," I retort. "It's just that I don't respond to names that are not my own. My name is Jane. Not Princess, not Princess Jane. Just Jane," I continue curtly, still looking down at my notebook.

"Okay. That's fair."

I stare at him. He's now looking down at *his* notebook, but looks up when he sees I've stopped writing. I am flabbergasted by his response.

"What did you say?" I ask. "Did you just agree with me?"

"Yep," he affirms. "See, when people actually talk to me and tell me what's bothering them, I tend to listen and change my behavior. Because that's what we're supposed to do as humans, right?"

This is what I mean by Preston's ability to look at people and just have a sense of what's going on with them. Because if he's trying to convey a statement about me not letting people know what's bothering me, he's kind of right. Haven't I been lying to my friends, lying to him even, about what's been happening with my family over the last week or so? Sure, he could have sensed my lies to *him*, but how could he possibly know what I've been saying to my friends? He can't, so he must not be talking about me.

"Yeah," I respond, "that *is* what we're supposed to do as humans, but if someone's okay with being bothered and decides not to tell anyone, then that's on them if nothing changes, right? It's their right to tell people, or not. Don't you agree?"

We've locked eyes now. For the first time, I get a good look at his. Very light green, with little flecks of blue in the irises. Lovely.

"Yeah, I do," he answers. "But sometimes when people do that, they take the risk of not only hurting themselves, but hurting those around them by their deception."

Deception. It's not a common word to use in normal conversation. So, he does think, or rather know, that I have lied to him. But even so, I decide that I'm not *completely* caught yet and will wait until he asks me a direct question about it before I embark on a course of action.

"Hmm," is all I say. And thank goodness it's all I have to say because our teacher has now commanded the attention of the room, ready to start the lecture.

Throughout the class, I swear I can see Preston periodically glancing at me out of the corner of my eye. Maybe I'm just imagining it. Or perhaps he's waiting for *me* to look at *him*, so he can look into my eyes with his own, reading my every thought and emotion. If that's the case, he's going to be glancing at me for eternity, because I am not going to invite myself to that.

The bell finally rings, and I fly out of my seat as our teacher yells out, "Don't forget, for homework tonight, read chapter twelve and answer the review questions at the end!"

I am the first one out the door. I enter into the quickly crowded hallway and am able to distance myself from the eyes of Preston Miller.

In my next couple of classes, my mind bounces between the events of the day, and my body is reminded of its exhaustion. I haven't slept well the past few nights. I lost two friends this morning. The excitement of the upcoming Ball has turned my heart into a million butterflies. And I lied to the only friend I have left. Then Preston Miller made his grand entrance into my everyday life again.

No wonder I can't keep my mind focused. My usual ironclad concentration is shrouded by sleepiness, stress, and the overwhelming feeling of isolation as I sit in my English class of twenty-nine people. My teacher is trying to lead us in a discussion about our assigned reading, but I can only hear short little bits of what she's saying. It's like the fluid between my brain and skull has turned itself into a thick fog, letting nothing penetrate – trying its best to protect me.

Thankfully I don't get called on in this class, but I really need to get this figured out. I need to be careful. Even though everything seems to be falling apart, at least my grades are still good. I've got that going for me.

This turtle of a day finally comes to an end, and people rush out of their classrooms as I trail behind. I don't dare go to Paisley's locker. Even if I made myself present and available to her and Lexi to apologize, I know they wouldn't. They can hold a grudge as tight as their high ponytails. Which, I may add, never fall.

I leave the building at the door closest to my classroom. It spits me out just a few steps away from my bus, which idles loudly in the bus loop. I climb the steps, take a front seat next to a window, and place my backpack next to me so no one can sit there. I lean my head against the window and try not to fall asleep as the bus eventually departs, taking its circuitous journey to the center of town.

When we arrive in Nana's neighborhood, I hop off first and speed walk down the road. I don't want to be reminded that I have no friends here as the others walk together, laughing and carrying on. I reach Nana's house quickly. I walk swiftly up the lane to the porch, open the door, and find Nana right where I expected, sitting in her recliner doing a crossword.

"Hi, Nana," I say in greeting, setting my backpack down by the antique coat rack.

"Hello, Jane. How was your day at school?" Nana asks.

"Pretty similar to any other Monday. It went slow, but nothing crazy happened."

Actually, a great number of crazy things happened, but I'm not about to tell them to Nana. She then does that thing that Preston does, looking at me like she sees into my soul.

"How was your day?" I ask her, falling onto the couch.

"Oh, just about the same as you," she responds with a small laugh, "nothing crazy, as you say. Though, my days have been very much the same over the past few years. I get up, get dressed, eat my delivered meals and do crossword puzzles. Although now that you all are here, I've been eating whatever your mother makes me, and save those other meals. It's been so nice having you all here."

"Delivered meals? What's that?" I ask.

"Oh, you know the people who send your friend Preston and his mother to my house to help me? Well, that organization also delivers meals to those of us who can't quite get around the kitchen like we used to. It's been so helpful to have that lately."

I'm a bit confused. I know Nana can't get around like she used to be able to; that's not what's confusing me.

"Is the food good?" I ask.

"Well, it definitely does the job," she says. "I've of course had much better but they're doing what they can to feed so many people. If the food's a bit bland, well that's alright because I am just grateful for the fact that I have it."

"Why don't you just order take out or something? That way, you can have really good food, even if you're not able to cook it yourself. A lot of places will deliver to you if you call."

Nana looks at me, searching my face as if she's trying to decide if I'm being serious.

"Oh, sweetheart," she says with a huff of breath, "if I did that for every meal I'd be out of money by the end of the week!"

"Oh…" I begin. I knew she doesn't have as much money as we do—anyone can see that by the size and condition of her house—but I hadn't realized she was *that* poor.

"Sorry," I continue. "I didn't think about that. I guess take out can get really expensive, huh? That is good, then, that they deliver meals to you. Maybe the rest of us can volunteer with them sometime!"

I need to redeem myself from my ignorant comment about her ordering takeout for every single meal. I still don't think takeout can be *that* expensive… surely if she's just ordering for one, it can't be that much. She's probably just trying to do that thing every old person does – they act like young people don't have *any* clue how the world works.

"That would be good," Nana says simply.

I lean back into the couch, closing my eyes. I hear the slight shuffle of paper and assume Nana has gotten back to her crossword puzzle. I think about how nice and relaxed I feel when I get an uncomfortable sense that something doesn't feel quite right. I sit up and look around, listening.

"Where's Scout?" I ask Nana, a slight edge of panic in my voice. It was the distinct absence of a certain someone asking me to play a thousand times that clued me in.

Nana looks at me over her puzzle, over her glasses.

"I think your mother wanted to be able to tell you that herself," Nana says mysteriously.

"Why? Is she okay? Why can't you tell me?" I shoot back.

"Scout is fine– I was just asked not to tell you where she is right now. And I'm not about to overstep on a parent's wishes. So hush. You'll find out in a couple of hours when everyone gets home," she says with finality.

It would seem I'm not the only one keeping secrets around here.

Over the years, I've expected my parents to not tell me *everything* – or, honestly, *anything*. They have their private conversations, whisper when they think I won't hear them, and all of their sneaky glances at one another over the dinner table. But I hadn't expected Nana to start to keep things from me, especially something as vital as the location of my little sister.

"Seriously?" I retort with a tone of blatant disrespect. I'm standing now, fuming. I can't help it. "Why is it *such* a big deal that I can't know where my sister is? I thought you and I were cool! Now you're taking my mom's side?!"

Nana looks at me, not with rage or disappointment, but something I can't quite put my finger on. Pity? Understanding? At the very least she doesn't look a bit surprised by my outburst.

"I think it would be good if you took some time to calm down, Jane," she says, calmly looking back down at her crossword. "I don't think I'm really the one you're mad at, so just take your time. I'll be here if you ever want to talk about it."

What does *that* mean? Of course I'm mad at her right now! In fact, the only person I'm *not* mad at right now is Scout, but only because I'm worried about her.

I storm away into my family's bedroom, fists clenched, closing the door much harder than I had consciously intended. I fall face first onto the quilted spread, my face as hot as a blazing inferno.

I hate everyone. All of them. I hate Lexi and Paisley for making a big deal out of absolutely nothing with Preston. I hate Preston for calling me Princess and then passive-aggressively mocking me for keeping my family's secret that I'm obviously entitled to keep. I hate Ashlynn for asking to come over to my house when I don't even have one. I hate my parents for not telling me *anything ever*, and Nana for going along with them.

It's not fair. None of it is. I deserve better.

I lie there facedown on the bed for I don't know how long.

Very slowly, I feel the normal color returning to my face. My heart rate slows down a bit. I'm still mad, but not as rage-filled as I was before.

My thoughts begin to become more rational. I don't know how long I can keep this up - this whole thing of acting strong so I don't get yelled at, trying to act normal at school so people don't assume things about me. Oh, wait. I guess I've botched that already by what I did this morning. It's not exactly normal for me to yell at my closest friends across the courtyard with the entire student body around me. *Why did I do that?* I could have just walked away and almost no one would have known.

And blowing up at Nana when all she was doing was adhering to my parents' wishes? Well, I don't think I should be blamed much for that one, because my parents' wishes are dumb. What is so bad about telling me where Scout is if she's fine? If it were *my* daughter, I wouldn't have skipped a beat in telling her *everything* exactly how it is happening. The truth.

I still feel bad, though, about yelling at Nana. She's one of the few people left that still likes me. Or at least I hope she does.

I stand and muster up the courage to apologize to her. I take a couple of deep breaths, which seems to clear my lungs of some of the heavy weight that this past week has placed there. I gently open the door and walk calmly down the hallway toward the living room. Right before I turn the corner to enter, I feel something lock onto my legs, and I almost trip.

"Jane! I didn't know you were home! Where have you been?" Scout exclaims in quick succession.

"Hey!" I say, much more brightly than I would normally greet her. "I was just resting in the bedroom for a little while. I'm glad you're home!"

She beams at me, like my reaction was all she has ever hoped for in her short four years of existence.

"Do you want to play dolls with me?" she asks, her lopsided grin looking up at me.

"Uh, yeah, for sure. I'll be there in just a little bit; I need to go talk to Mom. Where is she?"

"I think she's in the kitchen cooking!" Scout says matter-of-factly.

"Okay, great. Go get the dolls and I'll meet you in the living room in a minute, okay?"

I detach her from my legs and walk toward the kitchen as she runs away into the living room, most likely setting up the most elaborate pretend-play scenario that she has ever come up with, now that I have so enthusiastically agreed to play with her.

Mom is indeed in the kitchen. Her back is turned from me as she places a pot of water on the stove for what I assume is the box of generic macaroni and cheese sitting on the counter. Seeing her makes me mad all over again, but I'm able to contain it. I need to know where Scout has been, but I also need to see how she responds to me before confronting her about everything else, though I'm not even sure the full extent of it.

She turns around and sees me standing there, starting a bit as though I've scared her.

"Oh! Hey, Jane. I didn't see you there," she says, crossing the kitchen to grab the can opener for an unlabeled can of who knows what. She doesn't look at me as she opens it.

"Hey," I begin. It's probably best to ask innocently, without trying to accuse her of anything. It's like approaching a very high strung dog. Anything could set her off. "I noticed Scout wasn't here when I got home, and Nana said you wanted to be the one to tell me where she was today."

I wait. Her face turns a bit ashen, or even a little embarrassed, as she struggles with the can opener. But she doesn't make eye contact with me.

"Oh, yeah. Well, since I'm having to be gone all day, uh, to help your father find a job right now, and since we can't expect Nana to take care of Scout all day, we decided to, um . . . enroll her in a daycare," she says.

A daycare? But Mom *despises* daycares. Hasn't she told us a million times?

Without thinking ahead to her reaction, I spit out, "Why would you do that? I thought you hated daycares?"

As soon as the words leave my mouth, I know I've said the wrong thing.

Mom's head whips up from the half-opened can, scowling.

"Oh, yes, because it's my wildest *dream* to have my daughter in a daycare," she says. "Do you honestly think it's something I *wanted* to do?! I would much rather stay here with her the whole day but I don't have a choice."

The injustice of her response to me makes me lose it again.

"But WHY can't you stay here with her? I'm sure Dad is quite capable of finding a job on his own. I don't understand! You always make it sound like daycares are hell on Earth and now all of a sudden you're just *okay* with putting Scout into one?" I shout.

"JANE - there's just things you can't understand. Don't you EVER try to imply that I'm not doing what I think is best for my kids, for our family!" she shouts back.

"Then just *tell* me," I say, trying to change my tone to calm her and myself down. "Maybe I can help. You just seem really stressed right now but I don't understand why. You said we were only going to be here for a little while, so it just doesn't make sense to me why you put Scout in a daycare so fast... just tell me," I repeat.

As I spoke, her eyes returned to the can, her hands attempting to finish opening it. Was she even listening to me? She looks up.

"Jane. Listen to me. Your father and I have told you everything you need to know. I don't want you asking any more questions. It's not your place to decide what you're allowed to know. You're still just a kid, even though I know you think you're grown. Your only job is to stay out of trouble so the adults can handle what they need to handle. Now go find something to do. Dinner will be ready in half an hour. I don't want to hear another word about it."

I turn away slowly, shocked to my core. In fourteen years, my mother has only yelled at me about five times, but three of those have just been in this last week. I'm not sure what I have done to deserve that. How has she changed so much so quickly? Based on her response, it's clear that there's so much more that she's keeping from me. But now I know much better than to ask.

I'm now very worried about Scout. I've always been told that daycares are the worst. There are too many kids for the number of teachers, the kids aren't able to see their parents for eight hours or more, and it is complete chaos with kids just running around, throwing toys and hitting each other.

And aren't daycares, like, super expensive? It has suddenly occurred to me that if we're having to eat food from boxes and cans, we can't have very much money right now, even though my parents have always acted like we have. Although, perhaps they're just being *extra* frugal to compensate for Dad losing his job, even though they don't have to.

I'm not sure what to believe anymore, now that I know for sure my parents are keeping things from me. And if it's true we don't have a lot of money, then what type of daycare is Scout going to? Definitely not the nice, private preschool that Paisley's little brother attends. Is she going to be okay there until Dad gets a job? And at this rate, who knows when that will be?

I am holding back tears as I enter the living room to play with Scout, like I promised. With a house so small, I'm sure she would have heard our argument, but she's already rattling off what I'm supposed to do with my doll, smiling from ear to ear, like nothing out of the ordinary has happened. Must be nice to be so oblivious.

7

Dinner is subdued this evening. We eat our macaroni and cheese and canned carrots in silence – well, all except Scout. She's busy telling us all about her day at her new daycare. She, of course, is exuberantly excited about anything and everything. She doesn't realize that it's not a place she should want to be.

"–and we got to play on this HUGE swing set, and there was this boy that could swing SO high, and the lady told him to stop, but he just kept going higher and higher and I'm pretty sure he touched the sky, and–"

I assume my usual practice of tuning her out, because I don't want to hear any more of the unstructured, unsafe chaos that is her daycare. While I was playing with Scout before dinner, Dad came out of the bathroom and into the kitchen, where I could hear him and Mom whispering. Probably about me. What a surprise.

I realize Dad hasn't talked to me much over the last few days. During the day, he's been out looking for a job, but now I'm wondering if even *that* has been a lie that my parents have told me. He's been here for dinner each day, but in the evenings, we've all been doing our own things, which for him has been silently reading one of the many ancient magazines Nana has on her coffee table.

He doesn't seem to be on the outside, but I wonder if he's as high-strung as Mom is right now. I'm extremely hesitant to talk to Mom at all right now, for fear that even one word will cause her to flip out on me again. It might be okay to talk to Dad, but it'll be difficult to get him alone in this shoebox of a house. Maybe it's not even worth the effort to try and talk to him. If Mom is this stressed about his lack of a job, I can only imagine what *he's* feeling. He's just a lot better at hiding it from us. I thought Mom was good at that, too. I guess I need to stop assuming things.

As I try to sleep, it's proving to be another semi–sleepless night. You would think that by now, on the fourth night of this arrangement, I'd be somewhat used to this old air mattress and my dad snoring. But I'm not sure I'd *ever* become accustomed to it. I drift in and out of my dream world, that at some point places me in a vast, cold forest. There's a big swing set just like the one Scout was talking about. There are about fifty kids that *I'm* supposed to be watching, who are all running around and I can't keep track of all of them. Then, out of seemingly empty space, a giant, gray wolf comes bounding toward us. It starts attacking the kids with its razor sharp teeth, while tiny shrieks fill the air.

I awake with a start, my heart beating out of my chest and a sinking feeling in my stomach. I notice soft daylight peeking in through the window, indicating dawn fast approaching. I sit up quickly, edge around the bed, and see Scout sleeping safe and sound. Her little behind is stuck up in the air, a bit of drool escaping the edge of her lips.

I sigh with relief. A few seconds later, as I begin to fully awaken, I remind myself that there was never any wolf, that Scout's daycare would *not* be set in the middle of a creepy forest, and my brain was just playing tricks on me. It felt ominously real, though.

Giving Scout another glance to make sure she's still alive and breathing, I grab some clothes and silently open the bedroom door. I make my way to the bathroom to start getting ready for the day even though I know it's probably about an hour before I even *need* to be up.

I use the restroom, get dressed, wash my face, brush my teeth, and try to get my hair in some sort of order. I usually wear my hair down, but right now it's sticking up on one end like I was electrocuted. My hair straightener I got for Christmas is buried in one of the boxes in the moving van, so there's no way I can get to it. I decide to put my hair up in a ponytail, even though I look really grungy with one. I typically only wear a ponytail when I don't have enough time in the morning to properly prepare myself, and then it's clear to everyone that I didn't put a lot of effort into my appearance that day. But now, I'm too tired to care, even though I have plenty of time this morning to do so.

There's not really anything left to do before I get on the bus except eat breakfast, so I head down to the kitchen to see what I can make easily and quietly without waking up my family. I open the pantry, and am appalled by its state. There's hardly anything in there! There are cans of soup, cans of vegetables, little plastic cups of fruit, some pasta sauce, noodles, and random baking ingredients. But nothing for breakfast.

The fridge is close to the same. Just a random assortment of items that can't be made into anything resembling a meal. I guess Nana had really been relying on those meals being delivered to her. I just don't understand why my mom hasn't done any proper grocery shopping yet, seeing as how there's hardly any food here.

I sigh, slightly frustrated as my stomach rumbles, and go to the living room to sit on the couch. I spend the next hour doing absolutely nothing, just changing my body's position on the couch every ten minutes or so. Finally, I hear some movement, indicating my family has started to get ready for the day.

Mom walks into the living room and sees that I'm already dressed and ready to go. She looks as tired as I feel, which I bet won't have improved her mood from last night. So I don't dare ask her about what's for breakfast. Thankfully, she brings it up herself.

"I want you to start eating breakfast at school," she says.

Ugh, I hate what they serve at school for breakfast. Why can't she just buy some groceries so I can eat here?

But I've learned from my mistakes. I don't question her.

"Okay," I respond obediently yet apathetically. "I'm going to walk to the bus stop early today since I'm ready. I'll see you tonight. Tell Scout and Dad I say goodbye, too, please."

I hoist my backpack onto my shoulders and walk out the front door.

As I walk, I start to notice things about the neighborhood that I hadn't previously. In just the seven minutes or so it takes for me to walk from Nana's house to the bus stop, four cars drive past me and turn into their respective houses, like they're just getting home for the day. What are all these people doing out so early in the morning? It's so weird here.

Our old neighborhood had its own predictability that everyone unconsciously abided by. People to work and kids to school in the mornings, then quiet until the kids got back from school and the parents got home from work. No one sat outside on their front porches for hours, like the people do here. It's so odd. Over the weekend, when I was brooding on the front porch, I saw multiple people walking around, talking to one another, and going into each other's yards like it was the most normal thing in the world. Maybe it is for them, but I think it's strange. People are supposed to keep to themselves.

When I get to school, I debate on whether or not I should even go to the cafeteria like I'm supposed to. I *really* dislike the food they serve for breakfast. But my stomach is rumbling, Lexi and Paisley are side-eyeing me from across the courtyard, and Ashlynn hasn't yet seen me arrive as her back is turned, clearly telling a story to my two ex-friends who aren't paying her any attention. I can feel other eyes looking at me, too. Eyes that very much remember twenty-four hours ago when I made a fool of myself in this very spot.

I go inside.

I head straight for the food line without making eye contact with anyone else. I'm not *embarrassed* or anything, I just don't want to talk to anyone right now.

I grab a styrofoam tray then survey my options. As I suspected, nothing is appetizing. But I'm hungry, so I make some choices and place the food on my tray. Crusty 'french toast' sticks, plain yogurt, and a carton of white milk. I walk toward the exit to pay for my meal, when a thought occurs to me.

"Um, excuse me. I'm going to start eating breakfast every day for a while, and I want to make sure there's enough money in my account. Because if there's not, I'll need to tell my mom," I tell the woman sitting behind the computer.

"Go ahead and punch in your lunch number on the keypad, darlin', and I can check it for ya", she says kindly.

I do, and she looks at her screen curiously.

"Well, honey, it looks like you're on the free lunch program so you don't need to worry about adding any money into your account at all! That's good news," she says as if it wasn't the most confusing thing I've ever heard in my life.

"Wait, what? I'm not on the free lunch program," I say.

She purses her lips just a bit, then looks back at her screen.

"You're Jane Prince, yes?" she asks.

I nod in assent.

"Then, yes, you are on the free lunch program. It says here you've been on it for a few years now, since you first came to our district. So that means you get free breakfast and lunch every day, if you want it."

I forget I'm talking to an adult for a split second/

"But that doesn't make *any* sense! My family can afford everything we need, my mom just prefers that I eat lunch at school because it's easier than packing a lunch! Or, at least… I *thought* we could afford everything."

My face falls and looks away, the kind cafeteria worker looking like she doesn't quite know what to say to all that.

"I'm sorry," I say. "Thank you for your help."

"Sure thing, sweetheart," she says, and I walk away. I must not be paying very much attention because I walk directly into someone. My tray just barely avoids spilling its contents all over their shoes. In the second it takes me to correct myself, my endless questions about why I, of all people, get free meals at school disappears from my mind.

"Oh, I'm so sorry," I say, as I adjust the tray in my hands, scooting the cup of yogurt so it doesn't fall onto the floor. The kid I hit turns around, and I almost drop my tray again as I see who it is.

"No worries," Preston Miller says as he turns and looks slightly down at me. "Oh, hey, Jane."

I don't know why, but Preston calling me by my proper name annoys me.

"Oh, so you're actually going to start calling me by my name?" I ask, rolling my eyes.

Preston adjusts his ratty backpack on his shoulder as he holds his breakfast tray in the other, and laughs slightly, like he thinks I'm joking.

"Well, yeah. You asked me to, remember?" He's looking at me like I'm crazy. And honestly? I'm starting to feel that way.

"Oh, right. Sorry. Thank you," I say quickly. "Well, I better get to eating this before the bell rings." I step around him and find an empty table far away from where Preston has now sat down with his odd assortment of companions to eat.

I don't really know anybody who eats breakfast at school, except for Preston and some other kids I recognize from my new bus. But I don't even know their names, so I sit by myself. I eat my less-than-nutritious breakfast quickly, finishing with just enough time to spare for me to throw away my tray right as the bell rings.

I walk by the door to the courtyard just as Ashlynn comes in, and together we make our way to class, engaging in only polite small talk since our classroom is not far away. When we sit down at our desks, she starts talking about something funny her dog had apparently done the night before, but I'm not listening that well. In fact, I don't quite register anything that's going on around me until the announcements start, and one of them makes me catch my breath.

"—and eighth graders, don't forget that tickets for the eighth grade Ball start today! Just a reminder that they are $35 and will be sold at lunch. Thank you, and have a terrific Tuesday!"

Oh, shoot! I completely forgot to ask Mom about the Ball! And to take me dress shopping! Ugh, but with the way she's been acting the past couple of days, I'm not sure I'll have a good opportunity.

Our teacher has already launched into the lesson when I register that I haven't even gotten my notebook out. I quickly and quietly do, hoping that he doesn't notice my lack of preparedness for his class. I spend the rest of the period trying to focus, but finding it so difficult as my mind is trying to pull me in a million different directions. The Ball, my mom, my sister, Preston, my classwork, and the weird gurgling that has started in my stomach from what I'm going to assume were those questionable french toast sticks.

I realize I don't feel well at all, but I doubt that I'm getting sick. I've barely slept. We haven't eaten anything substantial at Nana's house, and now I have to eat *two* meals a day at school. My mom keeps yelling at me about things I have zero control over. Scout's at a daycare, probably being ignored by her teachers and getting beat up by the other kids. And what was that about me being on the free lunch program? That whole thing just adds to my ever-increasing suspicions that my parents are being frugal for frugal's sake, because I *know* we have money . . . right? I'm guessing they lied on the lunch form so I could get free meals to save money. That's definitely something Mom would do. It's the only logical explanation.

The bell rings, signaling the end of the period. I walk to Science, hardly noticing anyone else around me. I can now feel my pulse pounding painfully in my skull. Great – just what I need.

Preston's already at our table when I come in. I sit down next to him and take out my notebook. I guess I walked really slow in the hallway, because the late bell rings just a few seconds after I get situated.

"Good morning, class!" our Science teacher greets us with unnecessary enthusiasm for such a day as this. "I'll be coming around to collect your answers to the review questions you were assigned to complete over chapter twelve, so have those ready for me as I come by!"

My gut gives a lurch. I *completely* forgot about the homework! I barely even remember him assigning us anything! When did he say that? Did I write it down in my planner? Did I even *look* at my planner last night? I guess I didn't do either, because if I had, there's no *way* I wouldn't have done the homework. And Mr. Douglas is super strict about our assignments. I'll definitely get a zero. Oh, no. Oh, no, no, no.

"Jane, do you have your homework to turn in?" Mr. Douglas asks me as he takes Preston's work from him.

"Well, you see, Mr. Douglas…" I struggle to come up with an acceptable (and believable) excuse. I wring my hands in my lap. The pounding in my head grows more intense each second.

"Uh, I actually don't have the homework because… because my little sister started at a daycare yesterday, and she had a really rough day. She's only four, and since I'm her big sister, I'm usually the only one who can calm her down. So I spent the entire evening playing with her and making sure she was okay. And because I was doing that, I didn't have time to do the homework." A complete lie, of course, but hopefully it's good enough for him. "I'm sorry," I add for good measure.

Mr. Douglas surveys me, like he's at war with himself in his mind, trying to decide whether to stick to his usual zero-tolerance homework policy or give me some grace. He decides on a mix of the two.

"Well, Jane, I'm really sorry your sister had a hard time yesterday, but that doesn't excuse you from completing your assignments. That's not how the real world works. But, since this is a first for you, I'll give you full credit if you complete the assignment tonight, and have a parent sign it to show me that they're aware you missed doing it. Perhaps then they can be more aware of how you spend your time at home. I'm sure they could play with your sister for *twenty* minutes while you do your work, hmm?"

Even though what I said didn't happen, I very much agree with Mr. Douglas. My parents *can* take more of the burden of entertaining Scout. Why does it always have to be me? But it doesn't matter. What matters is that I got a pass for today… as long as I figure out a way to get one of my parents' signatures without them realizing that I didn't do my homework. They'd flip out.

Mr. Douglas walks away to start the lesson, and Preston leans over to whisper to me.

"Scout started at a daycare? I thought you and your mom hated daycares?" he asks.

"How did you know she hated daycares?" I ask, bamboozled by this random piece of accurate knowledge that just came out of his mouth.

"Oh," he says, looking down. "Well, Mrs. McCarthy – your Nana – mentioned it to me one time. At the time, I didn't know she was talking about you guys, because I didn't know you were related. She just talked about her grandson's wife, and her great-grandkids, but never names. She was talking about you and your mom, though, right? Or was it one of your cousins or something?"

"No, you were right, it was us. *Is* us," I answer. "My mom has always talked about not liking daycares because she'd be missing her kids' childhoods. I agree with her, but now all of a sudden she put Scout in one."

"Did she say why?" Preston asks gently.

Why the sudden interest in my family? I mean, I know he just found out that Nana was, well, my Nana, but he's asking questions he has no right to know the answers to. He doesn't need to know that my dad lost his job, that my parents are essentially lying to me, or that we're actually *living* with Nana, even if he suspects that last one.

"No, she didn't say. But I guess she just wants to get her ready for Kindergarten, maybe. I don't know, though," I say.

"Preston. Jane. Eyes and ears up front, please," Mr. Douglas says to us, snapping me back into focus, and feeling a bit embarrassed. I hate being called out by a teacher during class.

I laser my focus to the lesson, trying my best to forget about Preston's inquiries about my little sister and my mother's decisions. I should have told him off for prying, but I hesitated. *Why?* Was it because he called me by my name this morning, instead of Princess? Was it because he asked so kindly, like he was worried about Scout? But why would he be worried about her? He doesn't even know her.

But then I realize – it's because he was just being nice. Making conversation. Man, what is *wrong* with me? Why do I feel the need to bite peoples' heads off lately, even if it's only in my thoughts? Well, to be fair, it's not like I'm being treated the greatest. And now that I think about it, Scout and Preston are the only ones who have actually been kind to me over this past week. Everyone else seems like they're on a mission to upset me. Even Ashlynn did me dirty when she was Lexi's little carrier pigeon yesterday.

Whatever. I take the win of my unofficial homework pass and just try to make it through the rest of the day. That sounds easy, but my fatigue, hunger, headache, and annoyance with everyone around me and at 'home' is making that really difficult. And I swear, another thing going wrong might just send me over the edge.

85

8

When I get home, the only person there is Nana, just like yesterday. As much as I found it excruciatingly annoying that Scout would greet me with her squeaky little voice, I have to admit that after just two days of its absence, I miss it. And her.

I greet Nana, who smiles at me, then I go to the bedroom and sit criss-cross on the bed. I pull my backpack along with me, open it, and get out my Science textbook and spiral notebook. I quickly skim through chapter twelve, then flip to the review questions. I don't usually need to read the entire thing before I start to answer them. A lot are self-explanatory, or I can just go back and find the exact answer in a heading somewhere in the chapter.

I'm finished within twenty minutes, and I want to kick myself because it wouldn't have taken me very long if I had just done it in the first place. But that's not entirely my fault. Preston distracted me when Mr. Douglas was telling us what the homework was going to be, and then when I got home my mom went psycho and yelled at me. So, yeah. Not my fault.

Now I just need to do whatever I can to avoid setting her off tonight, so that she, or I guess Dad, can sign this. I'm no good at forging signatures, or else I'd just do that.

By the time everyone gets home, I'm starving and still tired, as my attempt to take a nap was rudely sabotaged by a particularly noisy bird in the front yard, who I'm sure was expressing his jubilant excitement that someone refilled the feeder out there.

I stagger out of the bedroom and try to make myself look pleasant, even though inside I feel like death. I can hear Mom bustling around in the kitchen. I don't dare disturb her. I decide to go into the living room, where I hear Scout's voice. It's different, though. Her usual sweet and high warble is subdued as she makes voices for her dolls. Something's not right here.

I turn the corner to see Nana in her recliner (of course), Dad on the couch with his head resting back and his eyes closed, and Scout on the floor with three of her dolls. Her hair is tangled like she just got out of bed, and her face is looking quite pale.

"Hey, Scout," I say as I sit down on the floor with her. "How was your day? Are you feeling okay?"

"Not really. I threw up and my teacher had to clean it up," she answers.

"Oh, no. I'm sorry," I say, surprising myself at how gentle my voice is. I don't usually choose this tone with her. "Are you feeling any better now that you're home?"

"Kinda," she shrugs, focused on her doll. "I fell asleep after and no one woke me up until it was time to go home. I didn't get to play on the playground with everyone else."

She says all this quite sadly. She must be in some sort of honeymoon period with this whole daycare thing, because I don't understand why she would like it there so much. I mean, they made her sick on her second day!

"That stinks, Scout. I'm sure you'll get to play on it tomorrow. Don't worry," I reassure her.

This seems to brighten her mood a bit, and she grins up at me, handing me one of the dolls. I take it with a smile, and start pretending that the doll is doing backflips. This gets a good giggle out of her.

Mom calls us all to dinner a little while later. When we enter the kitchen and sit at the small, rickety table, I can see that it's bean and onion soup for tonight's meal. Definitely not my favorite, but it looks like Mom actually made it instead of it being from a can. That's a plus. She places a loaf of sliced, plain white bread on the table (but no butter), and tells us to dig in. I do, and it tastes amazing, but probably only because I'm so hungry. While we eat, I see an opportunity to get on Mom's good side.

"Mmm, this is really good, Mom!" I say with an enthusiasm I haven't displayed in several days.

She eyes me a little suspiciously, but seems to think better of calling out my abrupt change in attitude right now.

"Thank you, Jane. I'm glad you like it."

I look over at Scout. She has curled up in her seat and isn't touching her bowl.

"Scout, honey, could you try to eat something, please?" Mom pleads.

Scout shakes her head and curls up even more, squeezing the life out of her doll that she brought to the table. When I was little, they would have gotten onto me if I brought any toys to the table, but Mom and Dad seem to have always had a soft spot for Scout... or maybe it's just because she's not feeling well... I don't know.

Mom sighs, but doesn't push her to eat anymore. The rest of the meal is silent, just like all our meals have been lately. I think everyone else feels just as tired as I do. I sneak a quick glance at each of my family members and see that exhaustion reflected. Scout, of course, is sick, so she doesn't look well at all. Dad looks like he could use a nap for the next week-and-a-half. And Mom – well, Mom looks like she just got back from war, judging by the bags under her eyes and the frazzled state of her usually-kempt hairdo.

How am I supposed to fess up that I didn't do my homework when they're in this state? And forget about asking for money for a ticket to the Ball tonight. I have a gut feeling that a plea like that wouldn't go well, even though it's a perfectly normal and reasonable request for any middle schooler.

We finish our bowls of soup, and I want more, but I can see from my seat that the pot is empty. I consider asking to finish Scout's bowl, but Mom is already putting it in a storage container and placing it in the fridge, just in case she wants it later. Mom takes Scout to the bedroom so she can get her ready for an early bedtime, so Dad and I go into the living room with Nana.

Dad and Nana start talking about the weather, so I just sit there and stare off into space until Mom comes back. She summons Dad into the kitchen so they can talk. Of course – because why would they want me to hear what I'm sure is a perfectly normal conversation? I am sick and tired of them being so secretive with us. Would it really be so bad if they had ONE conversation in front of me?!

I can hear the hissing of their whispers from the kitchen, and again feel the urge to go listen in. But I can't, of course, since Nana's sitting right there and would most definitely not approve. The injustice of being left out suddenly infuriates me. It's not just that they're not telling me things - it's that they're making a pointed effort to show me that they're not including me in the conversation.

Like, I get that parents *sometimes* need to talk to one another about things that don't involve the kids, but *every* time? That doesn't seem right or normal to me. I'm feeling that hot surge of anger that has come on so suddenly the past few days, and I don't know what to do about it. I can't very well yell at my parents, because it will just make *them* mad. As if they have any right to be.

They come in a few minutes later, and I uncross my arms and try to wipe the scowl off of my face so they don't comment on it. Both of them sit down on the couch and turn their bodies to face me. *Uh-oh.* This is what they do when they're about to tell me something bad. They're wearing the same looks on their faces that they did when they told me Dad lost his job and we had to live here for a while. Which reminds me - when is 'a while' going to end?!

"Jane," Mom starts. "We need to ask a really big favor of you." She looks at Dad, who nods, then continues. "You know how Scout isn't feeling too well this evening?"

I nod.

"Well, she actually threw up at school, and—"

"I know she did. She told me," I interrupt, somehow feeling the need to prove to her that I actually *do* know a lot of what's going on in this house, even if *she's* not the one to grant me that access.

"Right. As I was saying, since she threw up at school, she's not allowed to go back tomorrow, or the next day. She can't go back until she's forty-eight hours vomit and fever-free."

That's good, I think, *she's not safe there anyway. Obviously.*

Mom continues. "And since your father and I need to be gone all day, we're going to need you to stay home and watch her."

My immediate feeling is of confusion.

"But I have school," I say to them, like they've completely forgotten I'm in the eighth grade and not a full-grown adult.

"Yes, but you're going to have to miss a couple of days. It won't kill you to miss *two* days of school, Jane," Mom says, as if already preparing for a fight.

"It might not kill *me*, but it might kill my grades! I'll miss so much! And you know how Mr. Scott is about attendance, he'll be all over my case!"

Mr. Scott is our assistant principal, and he's extremely strict about attendance. Our school has one of the strictest policies in the city. It's something he enacted a few years ago when they realized kids were skipping school at an alarming rate.

"Jane, I think you're overreacting. Missing a couple of days is fine. You'll be fine." She suddenly gets a flash of anger, and I am shaken to my core as she drills into me, her voice rising to a shout. "And we're your parents! We're telling you to do something, so you better shut up and do it! Your sister is sick, and *you're* worried about missing school?!"

"Juliette–", Dad starts to say to her, placing a hand gently on her shoulder.

"No, George, she's sitting there freaking out because we're asking *one* thing of her, instead of giving her everything she wants!"

"I'm not freaking out," I begin, ready as ever to defend myself against the injustice of this tirade. "I just don't understand why *you* can't stay home and take care of Scout. I mean, you're her *mom*, and I have school! I would miss so much in two days, and it'd be so hard to get caught up with all my classes!"

Mom acts like she doesn't hear me, continuing her rant.

"You know, most kids would jump at the chance to miss school for a couple of days, but noooo, not you!"

"I mean, it's fun every once in a while to miss school, but we're starting a lot of projects, and I need to be there to get ready for them, and for tests and–"

"You better start acting like a part of this family – you're gonna start being grateful for what you are given, take care of your sister, and DO WHAT WE SAY! AND I DON'T WANT TO HEAR ANOTHER WORD ABOUT IT!"

Silence. Her words hang in the air like a sad, partially deflated balloon. I sit there completely stunned. My mind is blank. I don't know how to respond. There are tears welling up in my eyes, threatening to spill over onto my flushed cheeks.

I look away from my mother. I get up and walk slowly, my hands resting protectively in front of me. I step right out the front door, close it softly behind me, and sit down on the porch. *What. Just. Happened?*

In the past week, my mother has yelled at me more times than she has in the rest of my life combined. Now, in just a week, I've been forced to move from the house I love into this dump, my parents disappear every day to who-knows-where. I can't sleep. We're barely eating anything nutritious. My little sister had to start at a daycare. My mother is screaming at me for existing. And no one is telling me *why*. *Why* is all of this happening? Is it something I did wrong? Is it something my parents did wrong? Because surely one's world doesn't flip over completely for no reason at all. *Someone* is to blame for all of this. And I'm determined to find out who it is.

I can hear my parents shouting at one another through the closed door behind me. This upsets me even more. They never fight. I can't make out every word, but I can tell that Dad is telling her off for yelling at me, for being too harsh. Mom is yelling back, telling him how he has spoiled me all these years.

Am I spoiled? Am I just a rotten piece of human? It really is starting to feel that way.

After a few minutes, the shouting stops.

I hear the front door open behind me a little while later. I don't want to talk to either of them right now. All of this has been completely and utterly unfair and unkind.

Out of the corner of my eye, I see Dad's tall figure take a seat next to me. He doesn't speak for several minutes. We just sit there in silence, watching all the different kinds of birds flit and flutter around the feeders and birdhouses in the yard. The tears on my face start to dry.

"When I was younger," Dad says after a sigh, "I always knew I wanted kids."

Where is he going with this? I wonder. *Just go away.*

"I wanted to be able to show new little humans the beauty of the world around us. To teach them right from wrong, and to make sure they know just how important they are in making the world a better place to live. But how is one supposed to do that?"

He pauses, though I don't think he's waiting for a response from me. So I wait for him to answer his own question.

"Well, I have no Earthly idea how to do that. Not a clue. I've been taking this whole parenting thing one day at a time, trying to figure out what the right move is on any given day. To try and do my best."

He takes a breath, then asks me a question.

"I want you to be honest with me, Jane. Do you think that your mother and I have been trying to do our best as parents lately?"

I finally turn my head toward him. Is he really asking me that? Doesn't he know the answer I want to say, that it will hurt his feelings? But he did ask me to be honest.

"No," I say. "I don't think you've been trying your best."

I can tell by his face that he was expecting this answer.

"Can you tell me why you think that?" he asks.

I hesitate before I answer, and think. To what degree should I be honest with him? I don't want to insinuate that he and Mom haven't been doing a good job at parenting, or haven't been working hard, but I also want to tell him how angry I've felt over the last week. I've felt frustrated, mad, confused, sad, and disorganized in my brain because I've been left in the dark.

"I wish you and Mom would just tell me what's been going on. This whole thing hasn't made any sense, and I feel like you're…" I don't want to say that they've been lying to me. "…keeping things from me".

I wait for him to respond. To my surprise, he nods. He looks out at the quiet street, whose lamps have just begun to brighten in the dusk of the evening.

"You're right. We have been keeping things from you," he says.

I'm slightly shocked that he just openly admitted that, after all the effort they've taken to be furtive. I wait for him to tell me what exactly they've *been* keeping from me, but he doesn't say anything, as if he's deciding at this moment what he wants to tell me.

"What have you not been telling me?" I prompt.

"Your mother and I are ready to tell you, but not tonight. Everyone's feeling pretty on edge, wouldn't you agree?"

"Yes, but I'm calmed down now. I want to know what you've been lying to me about!" I nearly shout at him. I don't do it on purpose, but I feel more comfortable losing my temper at him because he's been so consistent lately. My mother has been all over the place with how she responds to me.

"I understand, but I would just like to ask this other favor of you tonight. Your mother needs time to calm down, and the two of us need to talk about what you need to know, and what Scout needs to know right now. I know this hasn't been easy on you this past week, and I'm sorry. But please, Jane. We need your help right now. We need you to take care of Scout tomorrow and Thursday, and I promise we'll talk to you tomorrow evening about it all. Does that sound okay?"

No, I think with an edge of resentment. *Just go get Mom and tell me NOW!*

I'm starting to feel angry again, but my dad's worrisome face stops me in my tracks. I know there must be many things troubling him right now, though I don't quite know what. I shouldn't be adding to his worries by being belligerent.

"Sure," I reply, trying my best to sound on board with this plan of theirs. I know he probably won't answer me right now, but I still have to ask, "But, I still don't understand why Mom can't stay home with Scout. I mean, *you're* the one who's looking for a job, right? Why is she having to be gone all day?"

"There's been a lot going on," he says vaguely. "But we will answer your questions tomorrow. For now, we all need to get some rest."

In what world is *that* an acceptable answer to a very specific set of questions?

He gestures for me to stand up with him, and we walk back in the house. Nana has disappeared, most likely into her bedroom. I don't blame her, what with the screaming match that went down. Dad goes to the bathroom, and I enter the bedroom. I lay down on my flimsy air mattress, still completely clothed. Mom isn't here, but I really don't care where she is at this point.

I suddenly feel completely exhausted. My heart is hurting, my brain is throbbing, and my face is still hot from the series of events that transpired tonight. As I drift off to sleep, my brain wanders to fantasizing about the eighth grade Ball. It's still something to look forward to, right? But as I begin to come to terms with reality, I figure that if Mom is acting this way, there's zero chance that I'll get to go. If my mother thinks I'm a spoiled brat, why would she let me go to something I want?

In the seconds before I finally fall asleep, I try to formulate what sort of questions I need answered from my parents tomorrow evening. But then I realize there's not nearly enough time in the world to ask all of them.

9

I awake late in the morning, strangely having slept better last night than I have in a week. My parents aren't in the bedroom, and there's no sound of any hustling or bustling going on in the house, so I assume they've already left to go job hunting – or wherever it is they've been disappearing to this week. I sit up and see that Scout is still snoozing away on her air mattress, her body sprawled out in the most uncomfortable position imaginable. Kids can be weird.

I'm glad she's sleeping, though. She needs as much rest as she can so she can get to feeling better as soon as possible. I still don't like the idea of her being at that daycare, but I also can't be missing school like this just out-of-the-blue. I wonder what my friends, or rather, friend, is thinking right now since I didn't show up.

The last time I missed school, I was out with a bad case of the flu. I think I missed maybe four days of school because I kept running a temperature. And you know what Lexi, Paisley, and Ashlynn did? They practically kicked our front door down on the second day to make sure I was still alive. See? It's like a national crisis when I miss. And it took me *forever* to get caught up on all my work. For the kids who aren't in advanced classes, it's probably not that big of a deal. But for me, if I miss even *one* day, it's not good.

I brush my teeth, then go into the kitchen to find a note on the table.

Jane,

There's frozen pancakes in the freezer to heat up for breakfast, and a couple of TV dinners for lunch. If Scout starts to run a fever, give her a dose of the medicine on the counter. If she throws up again, just clean it up and try to get her to drink some water. Nana got picked up this morning to go to a doctor's appointment but she should be back in the afternoon. Don't mess with any of her things and just keep Scout hydrated and happy. We'll be back around 5.

Mom

Not even a 'hey thanks for watching Scout and making sure she doesn't die!'? Nice.

I go ahead and heat up the pancakes from the freezer and try to enjoy them. It's difficult, though, as they're quite soggy since they were covered in ice crystals when I put them in the microwave. I feel exceptionally calmer than I did last night, although the crust on my cheeks would beg to differ. I must have been crying in my sleep.

Scout staggers into the kitchen as I'm finishing my last bite of pancake. She's rubbing her eyes with the back of her hand, and her hair looks like a bird made a nest in it.

"Hey Scout. Are you feeling better?" I ask.

She nods, but says no to the pancakes I offer to cook for her. I make them anyway, just in case she wants them later. When I sit back down at the table, she climbs into the chair next to me and curls up, holding onto my arm like it's her favorite stuffed animal. I look down at her, and see that her eyes have closed.

"Scout," I whisper," if you're still tired, maybe you should go lay down in Mom and Dad's bed. It's pretty comfy."

"Will you come with me?" she asks groggily.

She's being so sweet right now, so different from her usual tornado-like self, that I find it difficult to say no. So we go into the bedroom, I lay her down under the covers of the big bed, and climb in myself. She snuggles up right next to me. Her breath quickly evens to a slower pace, and I know she has fallen back asleep.

As I lie there, I realize that I haven't asked her how she has been handling everything that has been going on. I've spent time worrying about her (and being annoyed by her), sure, but I don't know if she's been noticing anything. Did she hear Mom and I yelling at each other last night? Did she hear Mom and Dad arguing afterwards? If she did, what did she make of it? Did she even understand what was said? Does she understand *anything* about what's been happening with our family?

I don't think I've given her enough credit for how stable she's seemed this past week. Other than getting sick, I guess. She has still played with her dolls, talked our ears off, and was strangely very accepting of having to go to the daycare.

If I had to guess, I'd say that since she's so little, she simply doesn't notice all the changes because she's just supposed to do what adults say. Little kids are used to that. They blindly follow their parents, even if their parents aren't acting normally. How would a preschooler know what's 'normal' anyway? And how would they even know to challenge it? Someone needs to step up on their behalf when they aren't being cared for like they should be. And in Scout's case, I think that person needs to be me.

The rest of the day drags on. Scout sleeps until noon, but still refuses to eat, even with my pleading. I'm worried she's not getting any better, and Mom will think I didn't take care of her today. But I've tried everything I can think of to get her to eat. She must be starving – she didn't eat dinner *or* breakfast – but even with me offering some candy I found in Nana's junk drawer, she still claims she's not hungry. I eventually give up, thinking that if she gets hungry enough, she'll eat.

Nana gets home in the early afternoon and sits down in her recliner, looking especially tired. I'm on the floor with Scout, trying unsuccessfully to come up with an imaginative scenario for the dolls so she will perk up a bit. I notice that Nana hasn't picked up her crossword puzzle. She's just looking at me and Scout, her eyebrows creased slightly, her hands folded in her lap.

"Everything okay, Nana? How was your appointment?" I ask politely, though really just wanting to break the tension that so surprisingly overcame me.

My question seems to wake her out of a deep thought.

"Oh, yes, dear," she says, blinking several times and smiling slightly. "It went well. Everything's fine. I thought I might have a word with you though, Jane?"

A word? Nana has never asked for a word with me.

"Uh, sure. Scout, could you give Nana and I a minute to talk alone? There's some bubbles out on the back patio you could play with. I'll be out there in just a minute."

Scout's too tired, or too nice, to protest. She nods, then gets up off the floor and heads in the direction of the back door. I hear the screen door close behind her, and turn to Nana.

"What's up?" I ask her, though right after I feel like that is too casual of a way to address my great-grandmother. She doesn't notice, though.

"I just wanted to tell you how sorry I am about what happened between you and your parents last night," she says.

This takes me by surprise. I thought she was going to tell me about her doctor's appointment, and that it just wasn't appropriate content for a little kid's ears.

"Oh. Uh, why are *you* sorry?" I ask.

"I'm not admitting fault," she replies. "I just wanted to let you know that I'm sorry it happened. And it wasn't right – the things your mother said to you."

"Oh. Okay. Um, thanks."

So maybe I haven't been overreacting with ruminating about the injustice of the things my mother said to me. If another adult (a very old one who has been around the block a few times), thinks that I wasn't in the wrong, then it must have some truth to it.

"Do you know why she's been so angry lately?" I ask her.

"I do, but like before, I have been asked by your parents to let them be the ones to explain themselves to you. I tried to convince them otherwise, but they have insisted that they are going to decide what they are going to tell you this evening."

"I really hope they tell me the truth," I say defeated, because I don't think they'll tell me the *whole* truth.

"I hope they do, too. And I think they will. But if you could, when the time comes for that conversation to happen, do me a favor?" she asks, waiting for my reply.

"Of course. What is it?"

"Whatever you hear from them tonight, try to put yourself in their shoes. Try to understand what it has been like from their perspective."

"Okay. Yeah, sure," I reply, wondering why this piece of advice warranted a private conversation.

"I do hope you understand me, Jane. Doing that – looking at things from someone else's eyes – is not a gift many people truly possess. People try to, all the time, but most fall short. That's why there's so much heartache in the world, wouldn't you agree?"

Okay, she's sort of lost me. I don't really know what I think about the source of the pain in the world. How is this supposed to help me with my parents? If anyone's not looking at things from someone else's perspective, it's my mom. She's just been ordering me around, or telling me off for this, that, or the other. She hasn't stopped to think about how it's affecting me.

I suddenly remember that Nana asked me a question.

"Oh, uh . . . sure, yeah. Yeah, I think the world would be a much better place if people, uh, did that. Yeah, I'll try to keep that in mind. Um – thanks, Nana."

I stand up and walk to the backyard. Scout is sitting on the edge of the rickety raised patio, tiredly blowing bubbles as she tries to keep her eyes open. I sit down next to her and feel grateful that she isn't up to talking right now, because I'm trying to piece together everything Nana said.

I don't understand why it would benefit me to try and see things from my parents' point of view when they haven't offered me that courtesy this whole time. They keep making decisions for me without any regard to how Scout and I feel about it. I've done my best to go with the flow – to spare them that burden of worrying about me – but isn't that their job as parents? To be concerned for my well-being? What have they done to make sure we're okay?! Nothing!

It can't be *that* hard to find a job, so why hasn't Dad gotten one yet? And where has Mom been disappearing to? Because I seriously doubt she's been helping Dad with finding employment, like she said. Or did she say that? I try to remember, but can't seem to recall if she's even told me where she's been going during the day. Ugh, I'm so frustrated! I can't *wait* for them to get home!

The rest of the day drags on relentlessly, and Scout is still declining any food or water. At this point, I'm thinking she needs to go to the doctor, but I'm afraid of how my mom will react when I tell her this. Maybe I should just let her figure it out on her own based on my report of the day.

I decide to tread lightly as they both arrive home, just in case they decide not to have that conversation with me if I do something that inadvertently upsets them. Neither of them seems particularly irritated right now, which is good. I stay out of Mom's way as she prepares dinner, and don't talk to her until she addresses me herself. I don't want to cut the wrong wire.

When she calls us to dinner, I'm feeling hopeful about my prospects of having a decent and civil conversation with them later. We're having chicken and rice bowls for dinner. I can't help but think how it's a perfect meal for an upset stomach — if only Scout would actually eat something.

As we begin to eat, Mom speaks to me across the table.

"How did today go, Jane?"

"It went fine. Scout didn't really eat anything, though. She's been really sleepy. I tried to get her to eat a bunch of times, but she didn't want to. She just doesn't have an appetite right now, I guess, from being so sick."

When I finish talking, I realize my heart is racing. I never used to be this anxious talking to my own mother, but now I feel like I'm walking on eggshells.

"Oh, dear," Mom says, looking especially worried. She looks intently at Scout, who has pushed her bowl away and placed her head on the table. Mom's eyes dart back and forth from Scout to my father, who also looks quite worried. And, of course, they're doing that thing where they speak without speaking. Then Mom seems to snap out of her own head.

"Thank you for watching her today, Jane," she says with a hint of her old self. The one who was so kind and gentle. It's so drastically different from how she's been recently that I stare at her. What's her game? Why this sudden change of attitude? Did Dad actually convince her that she needed to treat me better? Did something happen? Somehow I'm annoyed that she thanked me. But I stop myself before I respond with instinctive snark.

"You're welcome," is all I say.

"How has the job search gone, George?" Nana asks, looking at him over her bowl.

I can tell Dad wouldn't have chosen this moment for that topic to be brought up. As everyone else is looking at Dad, I sneak a look at Nana, who, I could swear, gives me the smallest of winks. Did she ask him this in front of everyone for my benefit? Knowing that he would be forced to answer, or else risk being rude to Nana?

He pushes his glasses up the bridge of his nose. He only wears his glasses when he is exuberantly tired, I've noticed.

"Yeah . . . actually, I was able to accept a job offer today," he says brightly, although judging by the way he shifts uncomfortably in his seat, he's not all that excited about the prospect.

A job! Finally! Now we'll be able to move out of this place and get a house of our own!

"Oh, that's great!" Nana responds with a similar tone, though with much more sincerity behind it. "What's the job?"

He shifts his body again, now pushing his chicken around in his bowl. He glances at Mom, who nods at him.

"It's actually at the factory. The one on the west side of town."

"The one that smells really bad and stinks up that whole side of town?" I ask without thinking, my face scrunched up in disgust.

"Uh, yeah. I guess," he responds, looking slightly ashamed. "The one that makes plastic molding."

Oops. I didn't mean to make him feel bad about it. It's just so much different than the museum. I can't help it – I have to ask.

"What's the job? Are you, like, an engineer or something?"

I would assume he's doing something that requires some brains. I mean, even if he couldn't get a job teaching or at another museum, at the very least he needs a job that utilizes just how intelligent he is.

"No. I'll be working on the line. It's an entry-level position, since I don't have any prior experience in the field. So I'll be shadowing somebody and learning how to do a lot of things first. But mostly I'll be helping the people who know what they're doing to make sure they have what they need to do it."

Well *that* doesn't sound glamorous at all. Nor does it sound like he's doing something that's in his wheelhouse of skills. He should be doing something with academics – with history, with art! Not *factory* work! I decide to add this to the list of questions I'm going to ask them after dinner, because suddenly Dad has become very interested in his chicken and rice bowl.

After dinner, Mom takes Scout to bed and Dad and I stay at the table, while Nana goes into the living room. We wait in silence for Mom to get back from putting Scout down. Dad takes off his glasses and rubs his eyes, the back of his neck, his head.

Mom returns, also massaging the back of her neck. All of this signals to me that they could easily be set off by any flicker of a bad attitude from me. I need to be careful if I want answers.

Mom sits down next to Dad, both of them facing me, the table between us.

"Jane," Mom starts with a sigh. "It has come to my attention that I have not been very fair to you lately. I want to start by saying that I am very sorry about what happened yesterday. I shouldn't have raised my voice at you. You were just wanting to understand, and I didn't grant you that opportunity to ask questions, let alone have any of them answered."

That's a good start. At least she apologized for what happened yesterday, even though she sounds like a robot. I'm just wondering when she's going to apologize for everything *else* she's done to me the past week.

"Your father and I stayed up very late last night talking, and we decided that you are old enough now to know the things that are going on behind-the-scenes with our family. You see, up until now, we've always tried out best to protect you from knowing the difficult stuff that goes on. We didn't want to cause you any worry, since you were just a kid."

"And we realize that in doing so – in keeping things from you – it hasn't really achieved that purpose," Dad adds. "I have never seen you so anxious and angry at us than you have been this past week."

Well, yeah, I think. *I've had plenty to be anxious and angry* about.

They seem to be waiting for my response, but I don't want them to stop talking just yet. So I sit there quietly, waiting for more. They look at each other, then continue.

"We never wanted to cause you any harm, Jane," Dad continues. "Please believe us about that. It's just with everything going on, it's been quite difficult to figure out what to tell you, and what not to tell you, while we've been trying to piece together everything that's been falling apart lately.

"And since you're so smart, Jane, so incredibly smart, we're sure you've started to piece together some of what's been happening. So, instead of us just talking, we wanted to let you ask whatever questions you need answered. And we promise not to lie."

"But we don't promise that we'll tell you *absolutely* everything," Mom interjects. "There may be some things that we still feel you don't need to know yet. But your Dad's right. We won't lie to you. We'll tell you if it's not something you need to know right now."

Wow. This is more than I had hoped for. I start to wonder what the final straw was that made them have this change of heart, but they're looking at me and I need to start asking questions.

"Can you promise you won't get mad if I tell you *how* I know certain things?" I ask, thinking about my eavesdropping of their private conversation last week.

"As long as it wasn't illegal," my dad chuckles with a big smile. I miss his smile. It feels like an eternity since I've seen it properly. I relax a bit.

"Okay, so I guess my first question is about what started all of this. What were those papers that we had been getting on the door?"

Mom takes a big breath, as if she were hoping for an easier first question.

"Those were notices of eviction," she says. "They were letting us know that we had to be out of the house within a certain time frame."

"Why did we have to be out of the house? Who was telling us to leave?" I ask. I don't understand how anyone can tell us to leave the house we own.

"Mr. Perry was the one telling us to leave," Dad says, placing his hands on the table, his fingers locked together.

"Mr. Perry?" I ask, completely confused. Mr. Perry is just a friend of the family. How in the world could he have the authority to tell us to leave our house?

"Yes," Dad continues. "Mr. Perry was our landlord. He's the one who owned the house. We paid him every month to live there, and he gave us a really good deal since I was his son's friend."

"*We* didn't own the house?!"

Dad shakes his head.

"No. We didn't. We rented it. We knew you thought we owned the house, and we chose not to correct you because we know how those–" he looks like he wants to say a not-so-nice word to describe them, "*–people* are in ValleyRidge. And we didn't want you to be ridiculed by them."

"Oh," is all I can think to say right now. But he's right, of course. If Lexi, Paisley, or Ashlynn found out that we were just renting the house from Mr. Perry, they would have judged me hardcore... just as I would have judged any of them if it were them.

"We thought we were doing what was best, though we can see now that we've just confused you to no end," Dad continues. "Anyway, we had been falling behind on our payments to Mr. Perry. He was very kind and gracious at the beginning, and even gave us a month free so that we could get caught back up. But we just kept missing payments, so he was forced to give us notice of eviction."

"And we thought we had more time than we did," Mom says, "but the day that you brought me the paper from the door last week was our final notice. He was having people come in to renovate the house, and he needed us out quicker. He had actually given us a lot more time to pack up and move than other landlords would have. But we were still taking too long, which is why we had to move so quickly last week."

"Okay . . . but what happened with the other house?" A memory suddenly resurfaces. "And who is Mr. Johnson?"

They both look at me, then look at each other.

"I overheard you talking in your room after dinner that day. Well, I didn't overhear. I snuck over and listened under the door," I say sheepishly, hoping that they remember five minutes ago when they said they wouldn't get mad at me for a confession such as this.

"Hmm," Mom says, looking a little upset but trying her best to hide it.

"Uh, yeah. So," Dad begins, trying to keep the conversation going before Mom flips her lid. "Mr. Johnson is the landlord of the house that we *were* going to live in. He was giving us a good deal on that one, too, because he knew my boss. But then, as you know, I lost my job at the museum. Then Mr. Johnson, of course, found out about it. We knew then we wouldn't be able to move in there, since I wasn't getting paid anymore. So we had to look for another place to go, and your Nana graciously agreed to let us stay here for a while."

He pauses and lets me process the insane amount of information I just absorbed. It's beginning to feel like I was living a lie that I didn't know I was living.

"Okay, so I get that this Mr. Johnson guy wouldn't want a family moving into his house when no one had a job," I say. "That makes sense. But I still don't understand why we couldn't just move into an apartment or something? Those don't cost very much, right? Then we would have had our own rooms and our own place, rather than basically living in a box."

"Jane," my mother says, as if I should already know whatever she's about to say, "we couldn't *afford* an apartment. We can't afford *anything* without your dad bringing home a paycheck every week."

"What are you *talking* about?" I cry, feeling my frustration levels rising. "Dad made *so* much money at the museum as a curator! How else could you have afforded to buy Scout and I name brand clothes, fancy dinners, and the trampoline?!" Nothing's adding up at this point. I can tell Mom's getting frustrated, too. But I can't tell if it's at me, Dad, or herself.

"Well, *we* bought some of those things, because we wanted you to fit in at school and in the neighborhood. It was a sacrifice we chose to make so that you would have a good childhood," Mom says. "But other things were…" she pauses, as though she wasn't expecting to tell me this part. "Other things were donated."

I can see a heap of tension leave her shoulders. She sighs, closes her eyes, and looks so defeated and small that I am shocked. Dad puts an arm around her, then continues for her.

"Jane, I wasn't a curator at the museum. I was on the custodial staff. I did the cleaning; I made sure the museum looked nice for the guests. I didn't make a lot of money. And since we decided to buy you some things that were pretty expensive, we didn't, and still don't, have any sort of savings. We've been living paycheck-to-paycheck for a long time.

"All your Christmas presents have come from the angel program at one of the churches in town, and your mother got a lot of your clothes from the thrift store because there's no way we could afford to buy all your clothes from the mall."

"So, we're . . . *poor*?" I ask, hoping we're not, even though what they said suggests we very much are.

"Well, if you want to put it that way, then sure," Dad says. "Now we're at this point where we're just trying to make it through. And we will, Jane. I promise we won't have to live here forever. But I won't start to get paid from this job for a couple more weeks, so in the meantime we're going to have to make sacrifices."

"More than we already have?" I ask, starting to get angry. "I've done EVERYTHING you've asked of me lately! I'm eating breakfast *and* lunch at school now which, by the way, I know now that I've been getting free meals from the school for years! I stayed home today to take care of Scout, I've slept on that *horrible* air mattress, I've eaten the disgusting food we've had for dinner, and I haven't complained at

ALL! *YOU* are the ones who have freaked out, not me! All I have done is ask normal questions and I've been screamed at!"

Fourteen years of being left out of conversations, being unknowingly lied to, and now recently being called spoiled and ungrateful have built up into this explosion of energy. I can't think straight. My blood is boiling. It's unfair. It's not right. I don't even think about what I'm saying before I say it.

"I can't *believe* you never told me any of this! Did you think I was that shallow, that I would care how much money we have?! I don't understand why you didn't just *tell* me? I would have understood! But you waited until we were about to fall apart as a family to say anything, and now it feels like you're expecting *me* to feel sorry for *you*! I'm not the one who forced you to buy me all that stuff! It's not *my* fault you didn't put any money into savings, yet here I am having to suffer because of it!"

I have hit a nerve. I've probably hit a lot of nerves, because Mom nearly gets out of her seat and starts pointing her finger at me.

"Now you listen here, Jane! You are just a kid! You have NO idea the decisions you have to make as a parent, YOU–" she's cut off by my dad taking her hand and pulling her back down to her seat. He's staring at her with tears in his eyes, and this brings her back from seeing red.

"Jane," Dad says calmly. "Do you remember our conversation from last night? How I asked you if you thought we were doing a good job as parents? Well we both agree with you. We know we have messed up over and over again, even if you didn't know about it until now. But there's nothing we can do to go back in time. Nothing we can do to turn back the clock and do it all over again. We have to keep moving forward. And I know we can say that we're sorry all day, but it won't change anything. But what we *can* do is try to do better by you and your sister from now on."

The silence that follows threatens to pull me into its darkness. I don't know what to say to that. Anything I say to counter it will reaffirm my mother's view that I'm an immature and naive kid. Thankfully, I don't have to be the first one to speak. Mom has regained her composure, and speaks in an even tone, but doesn't look at me.

"Part of moving forward is making sure every member of the family is doing their part to help get us out of this rut," she says. "So, it is very important that you do, sorry, *continue* to do everything we ask of you, Jane. There are going to be more sacrifices that need to be made over the next few weeks. We will stick with our promise that we will keep you informed on what is happening, if you can promise that you'll help out in any way you can."

While I still feel the slight pang of injustice that I'm having to sacrifice to correct their poor decisions, I suddenly remember the little girl sleeping in the crowded room next to us. She deserves better.

"Okay," I say. "I'll do what I can to make sure we can move forward. But I have one more question right now."

"Sure,. What is it?" Mom asks.

"Where have you really been going during the day that makes it to where you can't stay home with Scout?"

"I've actually been looking for a job, too – to try and get some more money coming in. The only thing I've found is a midday shift at the supermarket down the road and I didn't want to take it initially. I tried to see if I could find an evening or night shift, but there's nothing. So I decided I'm going to take that one. It's not ideal, but that's what needs to happen right now," she says. "And the past few days, I've also been going around trying to get us signed up for some assistance programs which help families like us who have been evicted, or are just struggling in general. It's been tough, though." Her eyes flit away, and I can see the tears making her eyes look like glass.

I had no idea. I had no idea about any of it. It's not my fault that I didn't know, of course, but I feel like I should have used more brain power to figure it out beforehand. But I'm angry with them. I don't care if it *looks* like they're trying. They aren't doing enough to fix what they've broken. It's obvious they can't do it on their own. They need my help. They need *me* – all of me.

I don't quite know what sacrifices the next couple of weeks will bring, but I'm determined that Scout will know none of it. I'm sure I'm partly to blame for the way things have ended up, but she sure isn't. She deserves an entire childhood without worry. And if my parents are off trying to piece together the mess they've created, the least I can do is make sure my little sister is protected. Because if I don't, I'm not sure anyone else will.

10

After our conversations last night, the three of us parted ways. Though truth be told, I couldn't tell you how the conversation ended, or how I even ended up in bed. My brain feels so packed full of new information, yet dormant, like it wasn't designed to hold it all and doesn't know what to do with it. This morning when I woke up, my parents were already gone, just like yesterday. I went to the kitchen to find another note from Mom, basically saying the same thing as yesterday. I didn't really feel like having soggy freezer pancakes again, so now I'm sitting on the couch, waiting for Scout and Nana to get up. Though I'm not sure I want the company.

I didn't have a ton of time to process everything I learned last night, since I fell asleep so quickly. Maybe I was just in shock, I don't know. Even though there was so much said, the one concrete piece of information that has stuck with me is the knowledge that we've always been poor, and it's my parent's fault that we got to this point of being homeless. *Wait, what?* The taboo word just popped into my head on its own. We're not *homeless*, are we? Are we? I mean, we certainly don't have a house, but we're not living on the street or in one of those sketchy shelters. We are in a *house,* but is it a *home?* It doesn't feel like one to me. No true home would make me feel like I've lost sense of who I am.

Scout comes into the living room first, holding her little arms across her chest and looking nervous. She's in her favorite princess pony nightgown, her skinny legs poking out of the bottom. She'll soon outgrow this sleepwear, and I surely hope I don't have to be the one to tell her she can't wear it any longer. She loves the ratty old thing.

She's walking toward me quite tentatively, as if she's scared to approach me.

"What's wrong, Scout?" I ask directly.

"I heard you and Mommy and Daddy talking last night after I went to bed," she replies.

I'm really hoping she didn't hear exactly what we said. Even if she could understand what has been going on, I wouldn't want her to know. She's too little to have to worry about any of that.

"Oh," I say, trying my best to sound like it was no big deal. "What did you hear?"

"I couldn't hear what you were saying but everyone sounded mad and sad. Are you mad and sad?"

I'm stunned by how intuitive she just sounded. Because that's definitely part of what I was feeling then, and am still feeling now.

"Oh, no," I say reassuringly. "We were just talking about school and stuff. No one's mad or sad, Scout. Everything's just fine.

Come here and sit with me for a minute. Is your tummy feeling any better?"

She looks a little less worried as she curls up next to me on the couch, but I can tell she's still not herself.

"No, it still hurts," she says, reaching down and hugging her middle.

"I'm sorry. Hopefully it'll start feeling better soon."

She hasn't thrown up at all, and as I feel her forehead I can tell she doesn't have a fever. Maybe it's just one of those stomach bugs that takes a couple of days to make its way out of your system. She's so pitiful when she doesn't feel well. I hate seeing her like this.

"Well, I think I know what helps upset tummies," I say alluringly.

"What?" She looks up at me expectantly.

"I have it on good authority that drawing with sidewalk chalk is the perfect way to make anyone's tummy feel a hundred percent better! Want to try it out?"

Her face lights up into the first real smile I've seen in days. She hops down, suddenly bursting with energy. We grab some sidewalk chalk I found sitting on the corner of the front porch, and spend most of the rest of the day filling the concrete walkway with color. We draw and draw until we run out of chalk. Scout seems to be feeling exceptionally better as the day goes on.

We haven't spent this much time together in forever. Even though I'm reminded several times throughout the day that I'm missing a lot at school, that we're more-or-less homeless right now, and that Dad has to work at a grimy factory, I find myself feeling quite at peace as I sit here with my sister.

When dinnertime rolls around, and everyone is home again, I'm ready to report that Scout has had a great day and is feeling so much better. But that changes when we sit down to eat. Mom and Dad somehow seem in more sour moods than they have been throughout this whole ordeal. I don't know what happened today, and although I do want to know, and they said they would tell me, I'm not really in the mood to be yelled at again. They said last night that they would try their best to tell me what I needed to know if I did my part, but I'm done asking questions for now.

Seeing their discontented faces only reminds me that they brought this on themselves. Why should I feel sorry for them when it's no one's fault but their own that they're having to deal with all this? And right now, I'm focused on Scout. She's suddenly pale as a ghost, clutching her stomach as she sits in her chair at the table. She's looking from me to our parents, wearing the same nervous look she did this morning when she thought something was wrong.

I'm the only one who notices this, because my parents are both working on eating their spaghetti while they talk frustratedly about the rise in gas prices. They are not paying an ounce of attention to their sick child.

"Scout, what's wrong? Are you going to be sick again?" I ask, placing my hand on her shoulder.

"I don't know," she says quietly, her face contorted in pain.

"It's gonna be okay. Let's go to the bathroom," I say as I stand up, gesturing for her to do the same. Mom looks up, finally, and asks us where we're going.

"Can't you see that Scout's not feeling well?" Nana shoots at her. I had half-forgotten she was at the table. "Jane's taking her to the bathroom because she's about to vomit all over the table."

Quite surprised by Nana's sudden defense of us, I quickly lead Scout away from the table, down the hall, and into the bathroom. I make her sit on the edge of the tub, with her head leaning over the toilet. I sit next to her and hold her tiny ponytail of hair back with one hand.

What was *that* all about with Nana? She usually seems so polite and amicable with my parents. Didn't she respect their wishes of not telling me anything? Didn't she get on my case about being more empathetic towards them? I wonder where this sudden change came from. She stayed in the house the whole day while Scout and I played outside, so I didn't really get a chance to talk to her.

Scout doesn't look like she's going to throw up anymore, but I can tell she's still in pain. So we sit there for a few minutes while I rub her back. Mom opens the door a little while later, her brow creased in worry, though lacking sincerity . . . in my opinion. How can she suddenly be *so* worried about Scout when just a few minutes ago all she could do was mope about the cost of gasoline?

"Jane, I can sit with her. Go finish your dinner."

"No, I can stay with her. It's okay, really," I say. I don't want her comforting Scout.

"Are you sure?"

"Absolutely."

She nods, then stands still in the door frame a bit longer than what someone normally would. She's looking at me with . . . what is it? Annoyance? Admiration? I can't quite read her expressions with much accuracy lately. She's been too unpredictable. She backs out of the bathroom, closing the door slowly behind her.

Scout leans her head on my arm, her breaths slowing down to a less panicky pace. I'm so worried about her. She ate a little bit of lunch today, thankfully, but other than that she has barely eaten *anything* the past two days. I know that at this point she desperately needs to go to the doctor. I guess she's technically allowed to go back to the daycare tomorrow, since she hasn't thrown up and she hasn't had a fever, but it's clear she's still sick.

I need to tell this to Mom, even though I'm sure she'll get upset with me for suggesting it when we clearly can't afford to take her. But none of us is a doctor, and that's what Scout needs. No matter how much it costs.

When some color has returned to Scout's face, I ask her if she would rather just go to bed early instead of finishing her dinner. She says yes, so I take her to the bedroom and tuck her in. She never actually got dressed today, so I just tuck her in, kiss her forehead, turn off the lights, and walk back to the kitchen.

Nana has retired to the living room, though Mom and Dad are still at the table. They've finished eating, but haven't cleared their plates yet, as if they were waiting for me to return. I've lost my appetite, though. I've worked myself up about having to advocate for Scout, and now I must actually do it.

"Did you put her to bed?" Dad asks.

"Yeah, she's super tired. I thought she was feeling better, but I guess not. We played with chalk outside for most of the day. Maybe it was too much and she wasn't ready for that yet. But I think she needs to go to the doctor. Her stomach keeps hurting like crazy, so something's wrong."

I wait to see their reactions, particularly Mom's, since she's been looking very close to snapping at the slightest provocation this evening. I wasn't fooled by her pretend concern for Scout in the bathroom. But she just sighs deeply, glancing from Dad to the table, to the wall, to me.

"Yes, I agree. I'll call first thing in the morning to see if I can get her an appointment at the clinic. Depending on when I can get the appointment for, you may need to stay with her in the morning, Jane. Would you be able to do that for me? I know you've already missed school and I don't want you to miss anymore, but I could really use the help."

She's actually talking to me like I'm not an imbecile, like she has respect for me. I didn't expect this at all, and suddenly feel guilty about thinking she was going to bite my head off. But her track record has been working against her lately, so no, I actually don't feel guilty. I'm annoyed that she's asking me to miss more school, but I have to remind myself that it's for Scout, not her.

"Yeah, sure. Just let me know in the morning, I guess. I'll get ready for school when I get up, though, just in case."

"Thank you, Jane," Dad says as he takes Mom's hand. "We really appreciate it."

"You're welcome."

We all stand, and I'm about to throw my spaghetti in the trash when it occurs to me that I should probably save it and have it later. Strange. Even though we've been poor forever, I suppose, neither one of them ever said anything about me throwing out leftovers before. I guess this was just one of those things they ignored in order to give me a "normal" childhood, like they talked about last night. It's an odd choice, if you ask me.

I shake away the thoughts of trying to comprehend my parents' questionable decision-making again, and put the noodles into a storage container and then into the fridge. I can have it for lunch this weekend, maybe.

Even though it's not nearly the time when I would usually go to bed, I decide to anyway. Playing with Scout all day has exhausted me, on top of the mishmash of emotions I've been feeling trying to figure out what to believe about my parents. They seem to be going out of their way to confuse me, honestly. Their actions have just been so inconsistent. Maybe it's best not to dwell too hard on it right now. I need to focus on making sure they're doing *their* part to make sure Scout is taken care of.

My head still swimming with a million plights, I drift off to sleep. I'm beginning to get used to this air mattress situation, like my body has started to accept its fate.

Suddenly, I'm somewhere familiar, though surprising. I'm standing in our school gymnasium, but it's definitely not suitable for basketball games right now. There's round tables with crisp white tablecloths, twinkly lights strung all the way across the ceiling, blue and silver balloons decorating the usually drab environment, and a hundred kids my age dressed in their finest clothes. There's an empty space of floor in the middle, just waiting for dancing feet to grace it with their presence. *It's finally time!* Oh, how I have waited so patiently for this day!

I begin to move into the gym, excited to see what everyone's wearing, what they're serving for the meal, and what music they're going to play. Something strange is happening, though. Everyone I pass is staring at me with what I can only describe as disgust, even though I feel myself smiling at them. What's wrong with them? What happened?

They're looking me up and down, then quickly moving away like I'm covered in porcupine quills. I run into the locker room, thankfully being right next to me, and find one of the full-length mirrors attached to the wall. I almost fall over when I see myself. I'm barefoot, wearing a bigger version of Scout's pony princess nightgown, and my hair looks like a bird has made a home in its waves.

I can't stay here like this. I dart out of the locker room, planning to make a beeline for the exit, when I run into someone. This someone is wearing a hole-filled t-shirt, tattered jeans, and scuffed up sneakers. I look up into the eyes of Preston Miller. I try to get away from him, but a crowd of kids pushes into us, forcing us closer together. They're laughing at us, pointing and snickering. My face is beet red – I can feel it. I look up into Preston's eyes, and see him smiling.

"Jane, you look so beautiful tonight," he says with true sincerity.

If I wanted to respond, I can't, because the crowd has pulled Preston into its depths. Now it's just me. I'm surrounded and they're closing in. Everyone's laughing at me. Everyone. I can't think. I sink to my knees, sobbing, as the crowd pushes in further, smothering me in darkness.

I awake with a start, tears streaming down my face, sweat filling my palms. My heart is racing, and I don't understand where I am for a moment. Then I start to come back to my senses, realize that I was dreaming, and my heart starts to beat somewhat normally again.

It was just a dream. Though it very well could turn into my reality.

11

When I wake up, I remember every detail of the dream I had last night. It felt so real. I can still remember the look in Preston's eyes as he called me… *did he really say* 'beautiful'*?* Because if anyone was the opposite of beautiful in that gym, it was me. It was so odd, and I don't quite know what to make of it. I shake the feeling away as I get out of bed and stretch my body. My muscles are very sore. Perhaps my body isn't as adjusted to the air mattress as I thought.

There's a hint of light outside, but the sun isn't all the way up yet, indicating to me that I've woken up in time to get ready for school and catch the bus. At least my internal clock is still functioning properly. Scout's still asleep, but I can hear my parents moving around the house as they get ready for the day. I reach into my suitcase to find something to wear, and notice that I'm almost out of clean clothes. When we packed to come here, I only prepared for about a week. And Nana doesn't have a functioning washing machine.

I decide worrying about the laundry is not a good use of my brain power at this moment, because I need to find out if Mom was able to make the doctor's appointment for Scout. I'm glad she's at least been able to sleep well this week. But she can't keep living with all these stomach issues. On top of the fact that I don't want her to be in pain, I really do need to return to school. And if she's not better, she can't go to daycare, which means I'll still be here taking care of her since Nana isn't able to.

I pull on my clothes quickly, and silently exit the room. I head to the kitchen, where my parents are both sitting at the table. Dad's reading the newspaper and Mom has her head in her hands, her thumbs rubbing her eyes in deep circles. I clear my throat to make my presence known as I sit down at the table.

They both look up and Dad greets me with a "good morning."

"Did you call the doctor yet? Can they see Scout today?" I ask Mom directly.

"Yes, I did. And yes, they can. I called right when they opened but the first appointment they could get her isn't until this afternoon, so I'm going to need you to stay with Scout this morning. I'm sorry, Jane. I know you wanted to go back to school today, but I've got my first shift at the grocery store, and now I have to ask them to leave early so I can take Scout to the doctor."

She says all of this rather quickly, as though she was anticipating me to ask these very questions about why she couldn't stay here with Scout. I give a deep sigh internally, but know that this is what will happen even if I don't want to do it. I accept my fate.

"Yeah, okay. I can watch her. Then you'll come get her and take her to the doctor?" I ask, in a way trying to make sure she knows what *her* job is today, too.

"Yep. It'll be too late for you to go to school for the rest of the day so you can just hang out here while we're gone. I was able to get some cereal and milk yesterday so you and Scout can eat that for breakfast, and then you can have your leftovers for lunch. I'll see what the doctor says and figure out something for Scout to eat after the appointment. Does all that sound good to you?"

I nod as she looks up, directly at me. For the first time in a while, I get a good look at her face. The transformation shocks me a bit, though I'm wondering if she's always looked this way, just less obviously than now. Her eyes have dark purple circles underneath them and her face appears sunken, like she's the one who is sick, rather than Scout. Overall, she just looks very defeated. Her shoulders hunch forward as she leans on the table, her right fist supporting her head as it pushes into her cheek.

As much as I am so very angry at her, and Dad I guess, for putting our family in this situation, I can't help but feel a tiny bit sorry for her. She must feel as lousy as I do, but the difference is that I'm just a kid. *She's* the adult here. She's the one who is supposed to make the good decisions so we don't end up like this. It's a lot easier to feel upset at her than my dad. At least *he* had a job throughout our childhood. I don't think my mom ever did, in the name of keeping us out of daycare.

I still despise the concept of daycare, but maybe if she had put me into one when I was little and worked in the meantime, they'd have some more money saved up and none of this would have happened. We wouldn't be living at Nana's. We'd have our own house. Mom probably wouldn't need to get a job because we'd just live off the savings they've built up, and Scout would never have gone to that daycare and gotten so sick from whatever mutant germs live there. But it's clear they didn't think that far ahead.

As they both head out for work a little while later, I realize that beside that one we had on the porch after Mom screamed at me, Dad and I have not had a proper conversation in a couple of weeks. He's let Mom do all the talking. I wonder if that's been his choice or hers. I'm angry at him, too, for everything under the sun, but then feel a pang of grief.

I'm losing him – the one who I could always count on to make me laugh, or to tell me something rather boring but at the same time super interesting about some old artifacts at the museum. Not that he was actually the curator. He was just the janitor. Maybe he's not as smart as I thought he was. *No. That's wrong.* He's still a very brilliant man, but not everyone has been able to see that. His boss certainly didn't, and whoever hired him for this low-level job at the plastics factory certainly doesn't realize that he could do something much more complicated than essentially being someone's assistant.

I honestly don't know what to think anymore. I don't know who my parents are, or even who they used to be. So much of it was a lie. I barely know who *I* am anymore. When I go back to school, will I even have friends? At this point, going to the eighth grade Ball is out of the question, absolutely. If we can barely afford food, how in the world am I supposed to bring up the topic of thirty-five dollars for a ticket to a dance? And forget about getting a new dress. No way that's happening. Just a few more things that my parents have taken away from me.

I'm beginning to envy Scout. She doesn't really have many friends yet, except for a few from our old neighborhood, but she doesn't seem to miss them. Sure, she's sick right now, but the doctor will fix her today. She doesn't have to worry about what people will think when she goes back to school, when she doesn't show up for the ball, or ruminate about strange dreams she's having about her lab partner.

Scout and I spend the morning playing with her dolls, which I've actually started to enjoy. Scout is starting to get really creative with the scenarios she comes up with for them. We're actually having fun together and being silly when that changes out-of-the-blue. We've been playing for about half an hour when Scout suddenly snatches the doll I'm holding from my hands.

"Hey, why'd you do that? I was playing with that one!" I say, keeping my voice light so she knows I'm not really mad, I'm just trying to make her remember how to share.

"YOU CAN'T TELL ME WHAT TO DO!" she screams.

Nana, who had been focused on her crossword puzzle, and I both look at her, quite confused. She was playing just fine, then out of nowhere just started screaming as though I tore the head off her favorite doll.

"I wasn't trying to tell you what to do, Scout, but you can't just take things from peoples' hands," I say gently, reaching over in an attempt to slowly and delicately take it back from her.

"NO!" she screams again. "IT'S MINE! GET AWAY FROM THEM!"

She hits me on the arm, fire behind her tiny little eyes. What in the world is going on with her? I'm prepared to start screaming back out of instinct, when Nana stops me.

"Jane, why don't you go get the mail for me? I need to have a word with your sister."

"Oh. Uh, okay. Yeah, I can . . . go get the mail," I say, standing up. Scout has gathered all of her rag dolls in her arms and is hugging them tightly, her body turned away from me. I leave through the front door and decide to walk slowly to get the mail, giving Nana enough time to give her a good talking-to.

That was so weird. Scout *never* acts like that. Ever. I decide that it must just be because she's still not feeling well, but I don't know. It was so sudden, so out of character for her. I'll just let Nana handle it, I guess. She's raised a few kids so she must know a thing or two.

I open the mailbox and there's only a couple of envelopes in it. They both look like junk mail, though, so nothing important. I walk back into the house, and see Scout sitting on Nana's lap, crying her eyes out.

"Scout, what do you need to say to Jane?" Nana prompts her, gently pushing her off her lap so she stands on the floor.

I instinctively crouch down so I'm at her eye level. She walks toward me sniffling.

"I'm sorry I yelled at you," she says pitifully.

"It's okay. Thank you for saying you're sorry. I know your tummy still doesn't feel good. That can make people say craaazy things!" I make a silly face on the word 'crazy', and this gets a small smile from her. She gives me a hug, wipes her eyes on her sleeve, and sits back down on the floor. She reaches for the doll she had taken from me, and offers it to me to start playing again.

I give a small laugh, and take it graciously. Throughout the rest of the time we're playing, I can't help but notice how completely opposite that interaction was than nearly every other one we've had since she's been born. I used to be the one snapping at her without provocation. She has always just been my annoying little sister who pestered me for the fun of it, right? Now I'm not so sure that's always been the case. She's just been herself. A happy, bouncy, sweet kid who only wanted her big sister to play with her. I haven't been fair to her. Not in the slightest.

And now, she's practically being ignored completely by our parents. I'm the one who's spent the most time with her over this last week. I'm the one who's been taking care of her, playing with her, trying to make her eat, and making sure Mom made her a doctor's appointment. I'm at least *trying* to make up for all the times I've ignored her over the years.

It really is a good thing that little kids' memories are short-lived, though, because the rest of the morning we play together as if nothing happened. In the early afternoon, Mom arrives to take Scout to the doctor.

"We'll probably be back in a couple of hours. Okay?" she says as she summons Scout outside.

"Wait! I want to come with you."

I'm not entirely sure what made me say it, as the last thing I want is to go to the clinic and risk getting sick myself. But I don't want my mom to miss anything. After all, I'm the one that's been with Scout this whole time, and the doctor might ask a question she doesn't know the answer to without my help.

"Oh. Are you sure? It'll be really boring," Mom says.

More boring than sitting at home while Nana silently does crossword puzzles?

"Yes, I'm sure. I want to come."

"If you insist," she replies, though it's clear she doesn't really want me tagging along. It's not like she has to keep an eye on me. I'm fourteen. I'm practically an adult.

We get in the car, and I make sure that Scout's strapped in her car seat as we drive to the clinic. It's not a very far journey, but as we go I realize that I haven't left the house since Tuesday. That's two and a half days that I've been stuck at home, with hardly anything to do but take care of Scout.

We arrive at the clinic, an old and falling apart building attached to a larger one that holds random offices in its depths. We get out of the car, and I take Scout's hand as we walk in. We've always gone to this clinic, but it never occurred to me before just what *type* of clinic it is. There's signs everywhere advertising free dental clinics for kids, free vision checks, free initial health screenings, stuff like that.

In the breezeway between the sets of automatic doors, there's a large display of various pamphlets on the left wall. I catch a glance at a few of them, but don't really understand what they mean. I see the words "Medicaid", "DHS", and "Cessation Program". I haven't a clue what any of that means, but I guess I don't need to if I've never heard of them before. But something tells me that if this is the clinic we've been going to forever, then it must be for all the poor people in town. Like us.

I take Scout to a chair while Mom checks her in at the front desk. I'm stunned at how full the waiting room is. There's a lot of little kids around Scout's age with their parents, some older people, and then a few people who look like they live on the street and just needed a place to sit and rest for a while in the air conditioning. I don't think I ever noticed this random assortment of people whenever we've been here before. I guess I just didn't think anything of it until now – until I realized what sort of family we are.

We may be poor, but we're not like these people. There's one mom who's not even watching her kids and letting them run around all over the place while she fills out a form. There's another lady that keeps coughing, not bothering to cover her mouth. Ugh. Disgusting. I pull Scout close to me and put my arm protectively around her while we wait for her name to be called.

Thankfully, we're called back quickly, because I'm not sure how much longer I can sit here. Scout doesn't seem to notice or comment on the strange congregation of people that had been seated before us. She probably isn't noticing them just as I never noticed them before in all the years we've been coming to this clinic. Little kids can be so oblivious to the world around them.

The nurse who called us leads us through a door and takes Scout's measurements. We're then directed into an exam room where Scout sits patiently as the nurse takes her vital signs and swabs her nose and throat. The lack of continuous chatter coming from Scout is proof of how sick she is. When the nurse finishes, she says that the doctor will be in shortly, and she leaves the room.

An awkward sort of silence fills the small space, as no one feels like talking. Mom is fidgeting slightly in her seat, and keeps checking the time on her watch. For some reason this infuriates me.

"What's wrong?" I ask her, not meaning to sound as disrespectful as I did.

Mom's eyes find mine, hers filled with venom. I know before she speaks that I should have stayed silent.

"My new boss at the supermarket said that he could only let me leave for a couple of hours. I just need this to go quickly. And anyway, it's none of your business what's wrong with me, thank you very much," she shoots back. "I told you to stay home but you insisted on coming, so just be quiet and worry about yourself, not about what I'm doing."

I stay quiet after that, not wanting to invite any more snake bites. I look over to Scout, who's lying down on the exam table, the thin white paper being crumpled and torn beneath her as she squirms around. Poor girl. I wish the doctor would hurry up so he can tell us what's wrong with her.

It's nearly half an hour before the doctor finally comes in, smiling at us like he didn't just make us wait forever.

"Hello!" he says enthusiastically. "I hear we've got a pretty sick kiddo on our hands. Do you know where I could find her?" he asks jokingly to Scout.

"It's me," she says as she sits up from the bed, holding her stomach. I see a hint of a grin on her pale face.

"Oh no!" he responds. "Well let's see if we can do something about that!"

Scout follows all of his directions as he examines her. When he's done listening with his stethoscope and looking into her eyes, nose, and mouth with the tiny light thing, he turns his attention to Mom.

"So, Mom, when did this stomachache business start?"

Mom looks even more frazzled than she did before. This appointment is taking a lot longer than she wanted it to.

"Um, well, she got sent home from daycare on . . ." she takes a while to answer.

"Tuesday," I offer. "She got sent home from daycare on Tuesday because she threw up, and has been home since then."

"I see," the doctor replies. "And has she thrown up since the incident at the daycare, or have there been other symptoms?"

Mom puts her hand on her cheek, and I can tell she's struggling to come up with the answer. Did she not listen to anything I've been telling her about Scout the past few days? Finally Mom looks at me, and I can tell she's giving me the permission to answer the doctor.

"Um, no. She hasn't thrown up since the daycare. She's just had a really bad stomachache. It seems to come and go, but she hasn't been wanting to eat very much."

The doctor nods.

"Has anything made it better?"

I think. "Well, yes. She was able to eat a little bit of lunch yesterday. We had been playing with chalk together for most of the day, and she always likes that. So I thought she seemed to be feeling better up until…" I stop, realizing that I was about to divulge that she started getting sick when our parents came to sit down at the dinner table. She had been fine when it was just the two of us, but I didn't make that connection until now.

The doctor seems to catch my hesitation but doesn't ask me to finish my sentence. He does, however, ask a direct question that I don't want to answer. Thankfully, he's looking at Mom and not me.

"Have there been any changes recently with her, other than the daycare? Anything going on at home? Anything that might be stressful?"

Mom looks even paler than Scout as he asks this question. I've never seen her so nervous before. I wonder why the doctor is asking this question; what does any of that have to do with her being sick?

"No, nothing that I can think of," she lies, looking away.

What?! How could she sit there and tell Scout's doctor that *nothing* has changed recently? Um, excuse me, the last time I checked, *everything* had changed! And if the doctor is asking this question, he obviously thinks it's important to know the answer! So why did she lie? All thoughts of being polite to my mother go out the window as my rage pours forth.

"Wait, actually a lot has changed!" I say, raising my voice slightly to make sure he heard me.

"JANE–" my mother tries to cut me off.

"No! He asked if anything had changed so why aren't you telling him how we lost our house, Dad lost his job, or anything else?!" I yell at her.

"I'm sorry about her," Mom turns to say to the doctor as she pinches my leg to get me to stop talking. That's always been our sign to behave if we're in public and she doesn't want to yell at us. But I don't care anymore.

"But Mom! He asked us the question so he must need the right answer to help Scout!"

"Okay, okay, let's all take a deep breath now," the doctor interjects. "I didn't mean to start an argument between anyone, okay? It's one of the questions I ask all my patients, so I don't want you to think I singled your family out for any reason," he says, addressing both of us. "Now, yes, the information you give does help me to figure out how to help Scout."

As he gestures to her, I look over and see tears streaming down her face. The doctor then sticks his head out of the room and calls for his nurse.

"Cathy, could you please take Scout to the hall really quick so I can speak to her Mom and sister? Should only take a second." He turns to Scout. "Nurse Cathy has the *best* stickers in the whole office. I'm sure she would love to show you and let you pick one out!"

Scout hops off the exam table, wiping her eyes. She takes Nurse Cathy's hand and lets her lead them out of the room. Once they're gone, the doctor sits back down in his chair and swivels to face us. He begins to speak in a very gentle tone.

"Mrs. Prince, it sounds like your family is going through a lot right now. I, of course, don't know *everything* it is that's going on, but I *can* tell that it is affecting everyone in the family in some way or another, as these things often do. First, you are NOT a bad mother, okay? I know that it can sometimes feel like you're doing everything wrong. It can feel like every choice you make is worse than the last. But I want you to understand me. I can tell that you care about and love your children very deeply. Do you believe me?"

Mom nods her head, as she frantically wipes away a tear that she couldn't quite hold onto.

"Okay, good. Because it's true. Now, about Scout. I could not find anything medically conclusive about why she's been having this persistent stomachache. But from what your older daughter told me, and from watching Scout during that last interaction in this room, I am inclined to say that her symptoms are showing up because of an excess of stress." He puts his hands up and shrugs slightly. "Now, is that conclusive either? No, absolutely not. There could still be a medical reason that her stomach hurts, but from what I have gathered from my assessment here, I would say that the stress could be a contributing factor."

He stops talking to let it all soak in, or to allow us to respond, but Mom seems to be frozen in thought. The wheels seem to be spinning in her head. We sit there almost a full minute before she speaks.

"Okay, so what can we do to help her get better if it *is* stress?" Mom asks.

I'm surprised she asks this. I half-expected her to get really defensive or deny that stress was making Scout sick.

"Well, since Jane said that she felt better when she was doing something she enjoyed, I'd encourage you to try and make sure she has time to do something like that every day. If you can spare the time, I think some one-on-one time with you could be beneficial. Let's see. Well, keeping some things as consistent as possible also helps young children to adjust to new situations as well.

"They can really thrive with structure, so a set bedtime and routine can help. I would try to be aware of any arguments that take place in front of her, if that's something that has been going on. I'm not saying it has, of course, but that's something that can really upset little ones and parents aren't always aware of how much their kids observe. I'm sorry. That was a lot of information all at once. Do you have any questions about any of that?"

Mom takes a deep breath, then shakes her head.

"No, thank you so much, doctor. I really appreciate your help. We'll try those things." She stands up to leave, and I can tell she wants to be out of there as soon as possible.

"Of course," the doctor says. "And if it's still not getting better in a few days, please bring her back and I can look at her again." He opens the door for us. Mom starts heading for the nurse's station to get Scout. As I pass him, the doctor stops me.

"Jane, I think you're doing a good job, too. When things get a bit crazy in our families, it's our siblings who we can rely on the most."

He gives me a small smile, which I return. Lately, I've been the only one who has been looking out for my little sister. And while

I'm not thrilled that it is basically a stranger, I'm glad someone else is sticking up for her now, too.

The ride home from the doctor's office is the tensest one I've ever experienced. I'm sure there's bound to be some repercussions for my outburst in front of the doctor, but I can't say I'm sorry I did it. I'm still so angry with my mother that she didn't answer the doctor's question honestly.

'No, nothing I can think of'. Seriously?! Maybe she was caught off guard because she wasn't expecting him to ask a question like that, but still. I'm glad I told him a little bit about what's been going on, because it turns out that all of it has been making Scout so stressed that she is in physical pain.

We pull into the driveway of Nana's house, and Mom tells me quietly to take Scout inside because she has to get back to work. As we're walking away, I hear the window roll down and Mom calls to me to come talk to her. I do, with Scout standing a little ways away in the yard.

"I want to talk to you tonight. Make time for me after dinner, okay?"

She didn't yell at me, yet, for what happened at the doctor's. I just nod, dreading what is to come of that conversation, and turn away from her to take Scout inside. I hear her car drive away, and I don't look back.

The rest of the afternoon is spent with Scout and I playing with her dolls (of course). I want to follow the doctor's recommendations, too – of doing something that Scout enjoys and spending quality time with her. Usually when one of us is sick, we just take some medicine and are better within a couple of days. But from what the doctor said, this is a whole different kind of sickness. I'm thinking it will take a lot to make Scout one hundred percent better from this. Though I'm wondering now if she'll ever be the same. If any of us will ever be the same.

12

I am dreading the conversation that is to come with my mother after dinner. Scout seems to get in a better mood as the afternoon goes on, which has made me feel a little better. But I know it's going to take effort from the whole family to make sure she doesn't get super sick again.

Dinnertime doesn't feel any more tense than it has been, so I'm not sure if Mom told Dad what happened yet, or if she's going to at all. I wonder if she's going to start treating him like the two of them have treated me all these years – cutting him out of the loop of knowledge to somehow 'protect' him from the weight of it.

After our meager supper, I linger in the kitchen. When the table is cleared, Mom suggests she and I go on a walk around the neighborhood since the weather is so nice. We go outside. I notice it's rather windy and chilly, and I question her definition of 'nice' weather. We walk around the neighborhood, and I shiver underneath the very thin jacket I grabbed on the way out. Neither of us says much for a long while, and I wonder if she is expecting me to talk first.

When I've decided I'm just going to suck it up and start the conversation, Mom speaks.

"So, a lot happened today," she starts. I don't say anything, and she continues. "I don't appreciate how you acted at the doctor's office this afternoon."

I stay silent, anticipating the lecture that is looming ahead. I knew she would say this, of course. She doesn't like to be embarrassed in front of people. Though honestly, I wasn't trying to do that. I just wanted the doctor to know what had been going on so he could help Scout. I gently nudge an acorn out of the road with my foot as we continue walking.

"I know all of this hasn't been easy on you, but there's no reason for you to be acting like that."

I stop walking in disbelief. *Did she really just say that?*

Mom stops a few steps ahead and turns to face me. I don't know where the courage comes from for me to say what I want to, but it happens.

"You seriously don't think I had *any* reason to act the way I did in the doctor's office? How about the fact that you were about to *lie* to your daughter's *doctor* about what's been going on in our family?!" My voice is raised now, and I'm sure Nana's neighbors are going to start poking their eyes through their windows very soon.

"That is NOT fair, young lady! You have *no idea* what I've been going through these past couple of weeks. No, that last fifteen *years* at that! There are so many things you don't understand about being an adult – being a parent – and the choices you'll have to make."

This sounds a lot like what she said during our screaming match on Tuesday night.

"But isn't it *your* fault that I don't understand a lot of these things? You and Dad admitted it yourself – that you had been intentionally keeping things from me all these years. If I don't understand something then that's on YOU!"

Mom looks like she's trying, though rather unsuccessfully, to regain her composure. I can't *believe* the things she's saying to me right now, but I need to calm myself down so she doesn't make me out to be this irrational teenager who can't control her emotions. I inhale a shaky breath, feel it rattle on the way out.

"I'm sorry about getting worked up at the doctor's office. I just thought that he needed to know all the information, since that's what he asked for." I try my best not to sound aloof or disrespectful, but unfortunately I don't think she detects any sincerity.

"Jane, it's not just that you got 'worked up'. It's that you told him, and were about to tell him more, things that could make it look like we aren't taking care of you two!"

This confuses me. I don't really feel one hundred percent taken care of right now, and I definitely don't think they're doing a great job of taking care of Scout. We don't have any clean clothes for tomorrow, Scout's been crazy sick, I'm having to miss school to take care of her, and we haven't had a fully nutritious meal in over a week.

"So, what?" is all I say, hoping she'll explain further.

Mom rolls her eyes and throws her hands up in marked frustration.

"*Because*, if someone even *thinks* we're not taking care of you in some way, they can call the state and send people to *take you away from us*. Do you want to get taken away?! Because that's what's going to happen if you don't shut up in front of people! Our business is just that – *our* business - and you don't need to go telling *anyone*, do you understand me?"

Right now, I *don't* understand. I thought kids only got taken away when the parents were hitting them or something. I don't want to believe that they would take us away for not being able to afford a house, or food, or a washing machine. But even though I don't want to believe it, when I look into my mother's eyes, I see something new. Fear.

"Okay. I promise I won't go around telling people what's been going on. I haven't even wanted to tell anyone, by the way. I just lost it in the doctor's office because I was worried about Scout. So don't worry, I won't say anything to anyone else." I didn't mean to come across as defensive, but I can't take that back now. I just need to see how she's reacting to it.

She doesn't say anything, though. She just gestures for me to keep walking. We've made a loop and are now back on the road that leads to Nana's house, the one that I walk on to catch the bus. When we're a couple of houses away from Nana's, Mom speaks again.

"I'm sure we'll come out of this soon, but in the meantime, please do your best to keep a good attitude, okay? Your dad and I have too much to worry about to have to come home to a snarky kid, okay?"

She touches my arm gently, as if to comfort me. "Thank you for all your help with Scout." She gives me a small smile, then walks us back to the house.

As I lie in bed a little while later, I feel a surge of indignation. Did she just criticize me then try to get me on her good side by thanking me? What *was* that? She certainly didn't seem to appreciate my help with Scout at the doctor's, or any other time this week. It's like she knew she was hurting my feelings, then tried to coat it with the sweetness of gratitude. Well, guess what? I can taste through to the bitterness quite easily.

I decide then that I am done trying to speak to my mother. If she's not going to own up to anything, then I'm not going to pretend like I care about the hardships she's going through. Evidently she doesn't care about mine or Scout's hardships unless it's to worry about herself getting in trouble with the state. Newsflash! I don't want to get taken away either, and I especially don't want that to happen to Scout. She's too sweet; a foster home would squish her like a bug. But I really don't think that'll happen. Mom's just being paranoid. Isn't she?

I drift into a restless sleep, trying to fight off the uncomfortable dreams that come to me. In one, I'm trying to figure out a combination to a locked safe that has Scout's dolls in it, while she stands behind me and wails. In another, I'm on a boat with Scout, a storm ripping us across rough waves and I don't know how to stop it. In a third one, I'm standing on a big stage while bright lights burn on my face. I can hear laughter. And I'm all alone.

I wake up with a jolt, though I stay completely still. My heart is beating hard, but not fast. My stomach has been doing somersaults in my abdomen, but is now still as a statue. Even after sleeping through the night, I'm exhausted. No one's in the room right now; they must have already gotten ready for whatever this dull Saturday has in store. I don't know what I'm going to do today, but if I had to guess, it'll be more of playing with Scout while my parents are off trying to get their lives back together.

Yawning, I reach down to my suitcase and rummage through, trying to find something to wear. Oh, right. I don't have any more clean shirts or pants. I pull out an outfit I wore earlier this week that doesn't look too horrendous, even though it's extremely wrinkly, and walk out of the bedroom. It'll be fine – we're not going anywhere, right? But we really do need to figure out how to do some laundry. I can't go to school on Monday looking like this.

My mind is still trying to wake up as I walk into the kitchen. I am stopped in my tracks when I notice someone standing by the sink washing the dishes.

"Mrs. Miller!" I say automatically, surely looking very surprised.

"Hi, Jane. It's nice to see you," she says as she rinses our dinner plates from last night.

"Sorry, I just forgot you come over on Saturdays. I've got my days all mixed up, I guess." A sudden thought occurs to me, along with a strange heartbeat of excitement that I wasn't expecting. "Is Preston here?"

"Yes, he's out in the front. I think Mrs. McCarthy asked him to plant some flowers she got delivered."

"Thanks," I say, and head that direction when I hesitate. Do I really want to talk to Preston? I'm sure he'll ask me where I've been, and interrogate me about what's going on. But I don't care. I need someone to tell me what's been going on at school, and it'll be nice to have a conversation with someone who won't yell at me or beg me to play dolls with them. I walk outside.

Preston is crouched down next to the side of the house, sitting on his knees. He's digging in the dirt with a rusty spade, bunches of little white flowers next to him, waiting to be planted. I watch him unnoticed for a minute. Little beads of sweat are dripping down his face, causing his long bangs to stick to his forehead. He's working with such focus; I can't help but admire him.

He looks up and notices me standing there.

"Oh, hey," he says, sitting back to rest on his heels as he takes a break from digging.

"Hey," I reply. "Uh, your mom told me you were out here and I just wanted to come say hi."

"Well, then 'hi'," he says. "What's that on your shirt?" he asks, gesturing vaguely at me.

I look down and am slightly horrified by what I see. There's several sizable red stains on my wrinkled yellow shirt, a result of my poor coordination from eating spaghetti several nights ago.

"Oh, uh, it's…" I'm struggling to come up with something, to make it seem like the shirt is *meant* to look this way, but I look up and see Preston smiling.

"Well, it looks to me like you had a wrestling match with some tomato sauce."

I return his smile, and laugh a little. "Yeah, it put up a good fight, too. I think I won, though."

"I wouldn't be too sure about that," he says with a brief laugh. "Tomatoes can be brutal. So," he continues, turning back to his work as I sit down on the porch, facing him, "haven't had a chance to go to the laundromat yet, huh?"

Laundromat? I've never even *been* to one of those before.

"Oh. Um, no. Not yet . . ." I trail off, looking down at my shirt again.

His comment takes me a bit by surprise. I have a feeling he knows more than he's letting on; that he knows what's going on with us. I suddenly remember my excuse for being here last weekend was that we were just visiting Nana. I knew then that he probably suspected I was lying, but I didn't know for sure. Well, there's no use pretending anymore, at least with him. I told my mom I wouldn't talk to anyone about what's been happening, but I feel an unexpected sense of trust for Preston. I know he wouldn't tell anyone. He's not a gossip like Lexi or Paisley or Ashlynn. Wow. I haven't thought about them in *days*.

"So, how's your break from school been?" he asks.

He turns his attention back to the flowers, as if he's giving me a moment to decide if I want to tell him everything, or anything. I think about it only for a second, then decide. I guess I have nothing to lose if Mom's going to find a reason to be mad at me no matter what.

"Yeah, about that. Um . . . I lied to you last week. We weren't, and haven't been, just visiting Nana. We've–" He cuts me off.

"You've actually been living here with her because your dad lost his job and your landlord kicked you out of your house? And you've been missing school this week because your sister got sick and you had to stay here with her while your parents worked during the day?"

I'm stunned into silence. How in the *world* does he know all of that?! I'm staring at him; I'd imagine with my mouth hanging open like a fish. He turns his attention to me, a hint of sadness behind his eyes, as if he's about to break some really bad news to me.

"I'm sorry," he says with a sigh. "Somehow Lexi and Paisley found out what has been going on with your family. I don't know how they know, but you know their moms are super nosey so I'm sure they did some snooping. And Lexi and Paisley have been spreading rumors all around the school the past few days while you've been gone."

I can feel a large lump forming in my throat, my head aching with pressure. How could this be happening? I knew Lexi and Paisley were upset with me, but I never thought they'd do something like this. Preston's looking at me with sympathy, or pity, or something else I can't quite decipher. Whatever it is, though, I feel comforted even though he doesn't say anything immediately. We sit there for a few minutes as I choke back tears. I take some deep breaths in an attempt to make them retreat.

"So," Preston starts quietly. "Is all of that true? Or did they make that up?"

I try to take a breath in through my nose and am met with the sound of a sniffle.

"Um, yeah. It's all true. I'm sure you knew some of it already though, didn't you?" I ask as I swipe away an escaped tear.

Preston looks a bit uncomfortable and looks away, but answers nonetheless.

"Yeah. I figured you were living here, but I didn't know why. It wasn't any of my business, though. So I didn't ask. But I did get kind of worried about you when you didn't show up for school three days in a row. I thought you might have needed to leave town or something."

"Why would we have needed to leave town?" I ask. I want to thank him for worrying about me, but it seems too awkward to do so. His last sentence doesn't make much sense to me. If he thought we were living with Nana, why would he think we'd have to leave so suddenly?

"Oh, well . . ." he pauses to scratch the back of his neck. "It's happened to us before – my mom and me. That's actually what had happened a couple years ago when we moved here. We were living with an aunt of mine after we got kicked out of our apartment. My mom had gotten behind on the rent so we asked my aunt if we could stay with her while my mom tried to find us another place. It had been going fine for a couple of weeks, but then she and my mom got into some kind of argument and she made us leave. And what were we gonna do? It was her house. So we left."

I'm taken aback by the vulnerability of this story he just shared so willingly. Does he really trust me that much? Because he certainly doesn't have much reason to. I mean, the people I hung around with are the biggest gossip spreaders in the school! I wouldn't trust me if I was on the outside looking in. But I'm also extremely curious for him to keep speaking. I've never known this about him, never bothered to wonder how he ended up here.

"What happened after she made you leave?" I ask. "Where did you go?"

Preston busies his hands with digging again, but answers my question.

"Well, we went to a motel first. It wasn't the most ideal place, but we didn't have any other family in the area. So it was our only choice. It was really dirty and I swear I saw a roach one night."

I shudder at the thought.

"Yeah, so we had to stay there for a couple weeks while my mom tried to figure out what to do. I didn't go to school that whole time, which is why I thought that happened to you. I'm sure we could have called the school and told them where we were so they could send a bus, but Mom was afraid they'd . . . *take action* if they knew how we were living."

Just like my mom.

"So anyway, she finally found a place she could afford here, which is where we're living now." He looks up as if he had forgotten I was there. "Sorry. I know that was a long story," he says with a weak attempt at a laugh.

"You don't have to apologize for anything," I say. "Thank you for telling me. That must have been really hard for you and your mom. I'm sorry that happened."

"Yeah, well." He gives a big sigh then leans back again. "I guess now you know a little bit about what it's like now, huh?"

"Yeah, I guess. But it's been pretty fine here. Nana's been great. I don't think I would survive in a motel."

"Well you would if you had no other choice. Give yourself some credit, Jane. You're stronger than anyone else says you are."

How does he do that? The way he speaks, it's as if he's inside my mind at all times. He can see into situations and just know and understand how people must be feeling. It feels a tad intrusive, but also so . . . comforting. I have spent the past two weeks feeling like an island, and he comes here and makes me feel at peace, like I'm not alone.

"Thank you." I don't know what else to say to his profound statement. I suddenly want to change the subject. "So, planting flowers today? Mind if I help?"

"That's okay, you don't need to. I can do it."

"Well I don't doubt that you can do it. I just thought you might want some company. Don't you always help my Nana by yourself?"

He gives a sheepish smile. "Yeah, I guess so. Well, if you insist. There's some extra gloves in the back of the truck."

I get up, grateful to be able to do something with my hands instead of attempting to process everything that just happened: finding out my friends betrayed me, the school talking about me, the fear that my mom will find out what happened, and the confusing yet pleasant feeling I get by being around Preston Miller. I pull on the gloves quickly and settle down on my knees to help.

Preston shows me how to dig a hole the right size for the flower bunches, how to separate some of the roots before planting them, and finally how to fill in the gaps without overdoing it on the soil. We set to work, side by side, the sun slightly burning the backs of our necks.

"What kind of flowers are these, anyway?" I ask as I place a bunch into a freshly dug hole.

"They're daisies. These are my mom's favorite kind of flower. She always says how they look like sunshine and clouds. Like you can have a piece of the sky on your front lawn."

I look down at the flowers and can see what Mrs. Miller means. The small yet long little white petals surrounding a bright yellow center. Sunshine and clouds. Shade and shine. They're perfect.

13

The sun beats down on our backs, warming my soul. About an hour later, we finish planting the flowers, then stand up to admire our work. They really do make the front of the house look ten times better; they are truly lovely. I look up at Preston, who is pulling off his gloves.

"Thanks for helping me with these," he says as he wipes the sweat from his face with the bottom of his shirt.

"No problem. I actually enjoyed it," I reply.

"You know, my mom and I were planning on going to the laundromat after we're done here. Would you want to come with us so you can have some clean clothes? I know that's probably why you're wearing a stained shirt, right?"

I nod, feeling a lot less embarrassed than I did earlier. Preston's just being so unbelievably kind that I trust him wholeheartedly.

"Yeah, I figured," he says. "I've been there. It's hard living out of a suitcase. Let me ask my mom if you can come, and you can ask your parents."

We walk inside the house, and Preston goes to the kitchen to ask his mom if I can go with them. I look around and realize that I haven't seen my parents or Scout at all this morning. There's just Nana, sitting in her recliner with her crossword puzzle.

"Hey, Nana. Where are my parents and Scout?" I ask her.

"Oh, I think they took Scout to the park. They told me to tell you that they'd be home later this afternoon."

"Oh, okay." At least they're trying to spend time with her. It would have been nice to get an invite, though. "Well, Preston invited me to go with them to the laundromat so I can wash some of my family's clothes. Would that be okay? I can take a load of clothes for you, too, if you'd like," I say, hoping my offer of altruism will persuade her to let me go.

"Oh, that's okay dear, there's people that come by on Wednesdays to get laundry from me. But yes, you may go as long as it's alright with Penny."

"Thanks."

I walk into the kitchen just as Preston is leaving it. He says his mom would love to have me join them. Elated, I go to our bedroom and start to gather dirty clothes into a mesh bag I find in my mom's suitcase. It's stretchy, so it easily holds the week's worth of clothing that we have accumulated. Though when I heave it onto my shoulder like Santa Claus, it almost pulls me to the floor. I didn't realize how heavy clothes could be.

I say goodbye to Nana and head out to the front with Preston and Mrs. Miller. We climb into their pickup truck, Preston in the passenger seat and me in the back with the laundry bag. We start to head out of the neighborhood, past the bus stop, and into the main part of the city.

"Thank you for inviting me to come," I say to the front seat. "I hadn't realized how much we needed to do laundry, and Nana's washing machine hasn't worked for a long time."

"Of course, honey, it's my pleasure," says Mrs. Miller. "I'm glad we could help."

Wow. I can't believe how *nice* both of them are. Sure, Preston used to always pester me at the bus stop and call me 'Princess', but when I asked him to stop, he did. And come to think of it, he's never been blatantly unkind to me. Well, I guess unless you count when he snarked about me living in ValleyRidge. But that was before he knew about how much we had been struggling. It was before *I* even knew we were struggling. And have been for a really long time.

So is he being so kind to me now that he knows what we're going through? No, I don't think so. I think he's just a kind person. Someone who is able to make others feel like they are the most important person when he talks to them. Someone you can't help but trust. I think about the large group of friends he always sits with at lunch. Sure, they don't match, and don't belong to one single social group at school, but they are all friends anyway. They're always so joyful when they're together. It surprises me that with everything Preston's been through, he has stayed that way. I'm also surprised that

I have been so observant of him over the last two years without even realizing it.

We pull into the cracked parking lot of a strip mall. The laundromat is on the corner, taking up most of the building's space. There's several cars in the lot, so we have to park at the other end. We hop out, and as I heave the laundry bag out of the seat, Preston offers to carry it for me.

"Oh, no that's okay," I say. "I think I've got it."

"For sure. You're strong, remember? But just in case, let me know if you need help and I'll take it."

There he goes again, being so thoughtful and… wonderful. I can't help but smile at his back as he leads the way for us toward the laundromat. When we enter, I notice long rows of giant, silver washing machines and dryers. Along one wall are some vending machines, an ATM, a coin changer, and a rinky-dink little claw machine. There's groups of chairs along the window covered wall that faces the front, and other chairs in the corners of the one, big room. The sound of the machines is near deafening, with so many going at once.

There's a lot of people here. Probably because it's the weekend and a lot of people are off work. There's people of all ages, but I do notice many families. Little kids keep themselves entertained on the floor with coloring books or little toys they brought from home. School-aged kids and teenagers sit at the few tables there are and work on homework. Parents, mostly moms, mill about folding laundry, switching clothes from the washer to the dryer, or sit watching their kids. There's some people that have chosen to use their time to rest, their eyes closed with their heads resting on the window behind them.

Even though this place feels so unfamiliar, I feel oddly calm here. Everyone seems so chill, like it's such a normal part of their routine that they are comforted by it.

We head over to a group of empty washing machines, and Preston starts loading their clothes into one while Mrs. Miller goes to the change machine. I follow his lead, and empty my family's bag into a machine next to his. But then I stand there, not entirely sure what to do next. I've never actually done laundry before, and I didn't think to bring any coins, which I now see the machine requires to function. I didn't even bring any soap.

Mrs. Miller comes back and gives some coins to Preston, then turns to me and puts some coins into my hand.

"Oh, thank you, Mrs. Miller. I can pay you back when we get back to the house," I say, feeling sheepish but grateful.

"Oh, don't worry about it, Jane. Have you ever used one of these before?"

I shake my head, and she begins to show me where to put the detergent in (which she also graciously supplied for me), where and how to insert the quarters, and which buttons to push. It's actually easier than I thought it would be, and once I press the big green 'START' button, I feel a great surge of pride that I accomplished this task. Silly, I know, but I feel like I achieved something wonderful.

"So, now what?" I ask Mrs. Miller.

"Well, this cycle takes about forty-five minutes to wash, so I am going to run to the bank while the clothes are going, and you and Preston can stay here and hang out. Does that sound good?"

"Yeah, sounds great, Mom," Preston says. "Could we have a couple dollars to get something out of the vending machine, please? I'm pretty hungry from gardening."

"Sure. Here you go," she says as she presses a few bills into his hand. "Just don't leave, and I'll be back soon." She walks away, and I'm left standing there with Preston.

"Want to go check out the vending machine? They have some pretty cool candies in here that you can't even get at the gas station," he says.

"Yeah, sure!" I say, following him around a row of washers to the wall with the vending machines. He's right, there are some interesting snacks in there. We both get the same thing, some spicy corn chips and a soda each, then go to one of the empty small tables to enjoy them and wait for the clothes to be done washing.

As we eat, I take a look around and observe everyone that's here right now. I'm a little surprised to see so many people chatting and hanging out with one another, especially since it doesn't look like a lot of them belong to the same family. Is everyone just that friendly to strangers? As I'm wondering this, an older, skinny woman with a near-balding head comes over to our table. Preston looks up and smiles at her.

"Ms. Petunia!" He exclaims excitedly. "How are you?" He's talking a bit loud, even louder than he needs to with all the machines going. I notice a hearing aid behind Petunia's ear and realize why he's doing so.

"Oh, doing just fine, sonny, doing just fine," she says with a toothless grin. "Who is this young lady? Is she your girlfriend?"

I look at Preston, and his ears have gone bright red, as my face does the same.

"No, we're just friends. This is Jane," he answers, smiling at her again.

"Oh, well it's nice to meet you, dear. Well I'll leave you two alone now. Gotta get Mr. Lawrence's pants washed!" she says laughing, turning away from us and heading toward the machines.

"How do you know her?" I ask Preston.

"Oh, she always comes to do laundry on Saturdays like we do. A lot of people here tend to come on the same days, so we've gotten to know some of them." He pauses to take a bite of chips.

Three weeks ago if you had told me I'd be sitting in a laundromat eating chips with Preston Miller, I'd have slapped you across the face for suggesting such nonsense. I'd have run in the complete opposite direction from any of these people if we happened to be crossing paths on the sidewalk. I feel embarrassed admitting that, even to myself. I'd like to think now that I've done a complete turnaround on that viewpoint, but I know that's not completely true. I'm still uncomfortable here, wondering just how safe I can be around people that seem nothing like me. I'm glad Preston's here, though. He seems so comfortable, like he's never known a stranger.

"They're good people, you know," Preston starts again, his voice lowered slightly. "A lot of them have just fallen on some hard times, and others have been having a hard time forever."

And there he is for the second time just today, saying something profound as if he can see directly into my thoughts. The intrusion impresses me, but doesn't allow the filter inside my head to work properly.

"Yeah, but how do we know who to trust? I mean, don't some of them do drugs and stuff?" I feel guilty immediately after saying that. I'm expecting Preston to reprimand me for being so judgemental, or at the very least stop talking. But he doesn't.

"Well, I'm sure some of them do. But no one seems to be doing drugs in the middle of the day at this laundromat, so why should I care?" He's smiling, looking down into his bag of chips.

I can't help but smile too.

"Yeah, I guess so. Sorry, I don't know why that came out."

"It's okay, Jane. It's not your fault. Don't you think people at school have said the same thing about my mom? People judge without even talking to you first. Just how it is." His smile has faded, and I feel the urge to fight anyone who ever judged the Millers for anything, ever.

Oh, wait. I did that, too. I assumed they didn't take care of themselves because they were too lazy or too unbothered. I noticed every day for two years what Preston was wearing, the state of his appearance, and his backpack, and thought that he just didn't care. Maybe he *does* care, but they just can't afford to get new things. I feel awful.

"I'm sorry," I say again, but this time it's not for the sake of the laundromat patrons.

Preston glances over to me, a puzzled expression crossing his face.

"I told you it's okay…" he starts before I cut him off.

"No. I'm sorry to you, and your mom I guess. I had thought really terrible things about you over the past two years, and that wasn't fair. I hadn't even given you a chance. I'm so sorry, Preston."

He's silent, weighing my words in his mind. His eyes pierce into mine as he turns his head to face me, and I feel that thing again, that pleasantness that starts in my chest and radiates out to my fingers.

"Thanks, Jane. That means a lot. I guess I should apologize to you too, then. I suppose the Princess of ValleyRidge has fallen from grace." He nudges me gently with his elbow as he grins jokingly.

"Ha, ha," I say sarcastically as I smile, though his words remind me of what I've lost. "I really do miss our house, though. Or, I guess I just miss having my own bed. The air mattress shoved in between an actual bed and the wall does not do well for a good night's sleep." I slump a little in my chair, feeling a bit down.

"Yeah, I've been there," Preston replies. "But it's not gonna last forever, trust me. When I was little, my dad used to always tell me the same thing whenever times were tough. He had a motto: 'No matter the chaos, the Sun will always shine.' It's pretty good, huh?"

"Yeah, that is good," I say, struck by another thought. "Preston, do you mind me asking where your dad is?" I have never seen his dad, never heard him mention a dad before now.

Preston's smile fades, as if he hadn't realized he'd let that word slip when he spoke. I hurry to reassure him.

"I'm sorry. You don't have to tell me if you don't want to. I was just curious because I always thought it was just you and your mom this whole time."

"No, that's okay. I guess no one ever asks me about him because I don't ever bring him up." He stares at his now-empty bag of chips, then seems to decide he can trust me. "He died when I was seven. So all my memories of him are from when I was really young."

"Oh, I'm so sorry," I say. And I mean it. Even though I'm not the biggest fan of my parents right now, I couldn't imagine only having one of them; having the other gone from this world forever.

"Thanks," he replies. "I don't know how he died, if that's your next question. Mom doesn't like to talk about it, which makes me think it was something really bad."

I feel a tightening in my chest, pained for Preston. That's just so awful. Preston's experienced loss that I couldn't have even thought of, yet he is so friendly, so helpful, so kind and generous. He was so friendly to that Petunia woman. He and his mom come over every weekend to help my Nana with things she's not able to do herself, and it sounds like they help other people as well. He invited me here and told me his story. He's chosen to be my friend, even though he had no obligation to. I had done nothing but be rude and off-putting to him, and he chose me anyway.

It feels good to call Preston Miller my friend. Because if what he told me is true about everyone at school spreading and believing rumors about me, he might be the only one I have at this point. That reminds me of what my mom said, what Preston alluded to earlier.

"Preston, you said earlier that your mom was afraid that the school would 'take action' if they found out you were living in a motel. My mom is afraid of the same thing if people found out we have been living like we are. Do you really think that would happen if people knew? Because from what you said it sounds like everyone at school knows."

He shrugs. "No. Well, I don't really know. There's some people I've talked to here that have had people come to their house asking questions because it looked like they weren't taking care of their kids. I don't know if any of their kids got taken away though. I guess it could happen, but I'd hope that's not true. Who knows, though? I don't know how it all works."

"Yeah, I guess that's true. I suppose there's nothing I can really do about it except not say anything else if people pry. Just in case."

"I wouldn't worry about it if I were you," Preston says. "There's people with much bigger problems than having to sleep at their great-grandma's house. What you *should* be worrying about is how you're going to make up all your work in Science class. I took some pretty good notes you can copy if you want."

"Oh, wow. Yeah, thank you. I'd love to copy them. Thank you for doing that."

I had barely thought of school the past couple days, other than coming to terms with the fact that I wouldn't be able to attend the eighth grade Ball. My gut lurches with the thought of having to face my teachers on Monday and ask for all my make-up work. It's going to take me forever to catch up.

Just then, a couple of buzzers sound.

"I think that's our machines. Come on, I'll show you how to work the dryers." Preston gets up and leads us back to our machines.

He shows me how to program the dryer, which clothes to hang up instead of dry, and offers to help me fold everything once it's all done.

The next couple of hours is spent with us talking, folding clothes, and sharing a bag of sour candy we buy with another dollar Mrs. Miller gives us when she returns. I never thought I'd be so content in a room full of rumbling machines and strangers, while doing one of the worst chores of them all. But I do. And in these moments, I feel something other than just plain happiness. I feel . . . bliss.

14

It's Monday morning again, and I walk briskly to the bus stop. I may be one of the only teenagers in the world who is excited to be going back to school after a three-day absence. I've just gotten tired of being cooped up in the house, and I don't want to get any further behind on my classwork, especially with it being so close to the end of the school year. But even though I'm eager to get back, I'm also feeling quite anxious. I don't entirely know what I'll be walking into when I get to school, seeing as how everyone apparently knows what my family has been going through, and has had multiple days to form their own opinions about me without giving me a chance to defend myself.

I try not to sweat it too badly, because I know that Preston will have my back. I think it's safe to say that he has replaced Lexi, Paisley, and Ashlynn for good. He understands me better than the three of them ever have combined.

After we finished at the laundromat on Saturday, Mrs. Miller drove me home and Preston helped me bring the clean clothes into the house, where the rest of my family had already returned. Scout was acting so much more like herself as she nearly knocked me over in an embrace when I walked through the front door. Preston said a polite hello to my parents and Nana, then told me he'd see me at school. That's the hope I'd clung to the rest of the weekend as I didn't have much to do at Nana's except keep Scout entertained. She hasn't had an upset stomach as badly as she has been, so she's going back to daycare today.

I think my parents were appreciative that I had done all the laundry, but they didn't react very enthusiastically. Mom, especially, acted as if this was something she had expected from me in the first place and didn't warrant a big display of gratitude. I was pretty sulky about that for a while, but I think I've come to terms with the fact that this is the way she's going to treat me from now on. Whatever.

Dad spoke to me a bit more on Saturday than he has been, but then on Sunday he wasn't home at all. Nana said he picked up an extra shift at the factory. I guess that's a good thing, but I've been missing him. I can probably count on one hand the number of hours I've been with him the past couple of weeks. I guess that's just how it's going to be with him now.

When the bus arrives at the school, I go directly into the building without making eye contact with anyone. I hold my head high though, not wanting to show any trace of embarrassment. I don't want to give anyone the satisfaction.

When I enter the cafeteria, I notice Preston right away. He's sitting with his group of friends at their usual table. I get my breakfast – today it's some sort of sorry excuse for biscuits and gravy – and make my way to an empty table. I know Preston and I are friends now, but I don't want to intrude on his group without an invitation. Preston notices me and waves me over, pulling an empty chair toward him. Thank goodness. I really didn't want to sit alone again.

I place my tray on the table and sit in the empty chair to the right of Preston. Besides the two of us, there's four other people seated at the table. I don't know any of their names, but it's a good thing Preston can typically read my mind, because he starts introducing them to me.

"Everyone, this is Jane. Jane, this is Braxton, Stacy, Lucas, and Brian," he says as he motions to each one in clockwise order. Most of them nod and smile, greeting me while they continue eating, except one. Stacy, the only other girl at the table, is eyeing me suspiciously with her arms crossed over her chest. She's leaning back in her chair, and her fork stabs her biscuit forcefully, as though she's trying her best to keep the utensil out of my neck. I make eye contact with her, then look down quickly. *What is her problem?*

Preston notices, too.

"Stacy, what's wrong?" he asks innocently.

"*She's* what's wrong," Stacy replies as she points at me with her fork. "Why is *she* here? What, do you have a meeting with your *besties* after this so you can make fun of us?"

"No, I–" I begin before she cuts me off.

"Because if that's the case then you can clear out now, ValleyRidge."

"Hey, lay off, Stacy. What's your problem?" Preston defends.

"Why is she sitting with us all of a sudden? I know what she and those other preppy girls talk about behind everyone's backs. They're horrible people, Preston. How do we know she won't do that to us? Is this some kind of joke?" Stacy's leaning forward now, her eyes filled with hatred.

"Stacy, shut up. She's not like them. She's cool. Give her a chance, will you?" Preston shoots back. I'm sitting there awkwardly as I witness the exchange. The other boys seem caught off guard by Stacy's outburst, sure, but it also seems as if she's done this before. I can tell by the way they've become hyper-focused on their meal, letting Preston take the hits.

"Um, I'm really sorry if I ever did anything to offend or upset you," I say. "But I literally did not even know your name until two minutes ago, I swear. And I've never made fun of *any* of you. I promise." I think it'd be good to try and get on Stacy's good side as much as I can. "But I'm really sorry if anyone else has ever made fun of you behind your back. For real, that's not cool."

My apology seems to placate her for a second as she absorbs what I've said, though I can tell she's trying to figure out if she believes me or not.

"Oh, and by the way," I begin again, "I'm not friends with any of them. Not anymore, at least." My expression changes as I say it out loud for the first time since Preston told me what they did last week. Lexi and Paisley, and I'm sure Ashlynn joined in, told the whole school my business because they were mad at me. No other reason. They just wanted to hurt me. So no, I'm not their friend anymore.

"Really?" Stacy asks, a trace of unbelief in her voice, though her body language suggests she feels some sympathy for me. She's leaned back into her chair and her face has softened slightly.

"Yeah, really. Though at this point, I'm not sure if they were ever my friends in the first place." I poke at my stale biscuit as a short silence falls over the table.

"Yeah, some of us heard what they were saying about your family," the boy named Braxton pipes in. I look up at him as he continues to speak. "But if they were trying to embarrass you or make you look bad, then the joke's on them because guess what?" he asks.

"What?" I ask nervously.

"Do you know how many of us have had our parents lose their jobs? Everyone, raise your hand if one of your parents has ever lost their job." He looks expectantly at the table.

Everyone raises a hand.

"Okay, now raise your hand if you've ever been kicked out of your place?" Braxton continues.

Preston, Braxton, Stacy, and Brian raise their hands.

"And now raise your hand if any of that made you uncool in any way.

No hands are raised.

"See?" Braxton says. "Sure, it can feel really embarrassing at the time, especially if you've known differently. But listen, that's their problem. Not yours. If they want to be jerks and try to make you look bad in front of everyone, then I think they've got their own issues to deal with."

Surprisingly, I feel comforted by this stranger's words. I'm not as alone as I thought I was.   "See? You don't need those girls," Preston says. "You've got us now. Right, guys?"

The three other boys nod their heads in assent, and I look around, overwhelmingly grateful. My eyes meet Stacy's and I see that she is still quite apprehensive.

"Stacy?" Preston asks. "Doesn't Jane have us now?" We all look at her.

She sighs and seems to make up her mind.

"Well, as long as you don't do something idiotic, then yeah. Don't go putting a tiara on your head and then act like you run the place."

I start to become slightly offended until I see her smirking at me. I return a small smile and get to work eating my breakfast before the bell rings. The rest of the meal, I listen as Preston leads a lively debate about whether or not our principal wears a fake hairpiece. By the time the bell rings, I realize that I am laughing, actually laughing, for the first time in weeks.

I'm in an exceptionally good mood as I make my way to first period, before I realize that I'm going to have to face Ashlynn. When I walk into the classroom, she is already sitting in her seat. I slide into mine across the aisle. I don't think I want to talk to her, but still find myself trying to catch her eye. She seems adamant about *not* wanting to catch mine, and keeps her eyes focused intently on her blank notebook, pretending to write something down.

A few weeks ago, I would have spiraled quickly if Ashlynn was giving me the silent treatment. But now that I've got someone in my life who's *actually* a good friend, I can see her immaturity from a mile away. As she refuses to look at me, my memory takes me back to so many of my interactions with my old friend group.

They seldom ever actually listened to one another, except for when they were making fun of someone else. They talked about themselves constantly without taking the time to acknowledge anyone else in the conversation. Even the last time I spoke to Ashlynn, at lunch last week, she just kept going on and on about herself when she *knew* how hurt I felt by Lexi and Paisley.

Was I like that too? Did I only ever talk about *myself?* And while I did make a conscious effort to abstain from joining their gossip, did I ever do anything to correct it, or tell them off? Nope. I think about the conversation at the breakfast table. Stacy wasn't being super nice to me, but Preston immediately called her out on it. Then they moved on like nothing had happened once it was all over. They're still friends. It's amazing to me how normal that was for them.

I shake my head slightly to clear it of my attempt to analyze a lifetime of friendships and try my best to listen to the Monday announcements. The woman over the speaker is reminding the eighth graders about the ticket sales for the Ball.

I remember how excited I was last week when it was announced, how much I dreamt about going. I've pretty much accepted the reality that I won't be able to go, but wow, do I still want to. Getting all dressed up, eating fancy food, and dancing with… my brain shows me Preston, dressed to the nines in a black tuxedo. But it was only an instant. Even if I wanted to go to the Ball with Preston, it won't happen. There's no way we can afford a ticket, so I push the thought out of my mind. It's not worth devoting energy to fantasies like that.

When the announcements end, class starts and I do my best to focus on the lecture, since I missed a few when I was gone. I hope reading the textbook will be enough to help me do well on the next test, but I don't know. It's all I can really do at this point, since there's no way I'm asking Ashlynn to copy her notes from last week.

The bell sounds signaling the end of the lesson, and I head to Science, excited that I'll get to be with Preston. When we're all settled, and Preston hands me the notes from last week that he copied for me, our teacher announces that we're doing a lab today. We're to go around the school with cotton swabs and try to find the dirtiest place we can think of. Then we'll come back and spread the swabs on agar to see whose grows the most colonies. Kind of gross, but it sounds like so much fun! We're to work with our lab partner, so Preston and I get our supplies and walk out into the hallway.

"Any ideas on what we should swab?" he asks.

"Hmm, maybe something in the gym? I doubt any of the football guys ever clean their helmets," I say with a grimace.

"Sounds like a plan," Preston responds enthusiastically.

We head down to the gym and Preston offers to go and swab one of the helmets from inside the boys' locker room. I tell him to go ahead, and I wait right outside the door. He comes back a few minutes later, placing the swab in the small test tube filled with solution that we were given.

"Well, that was disgusting. I think we have a good chance of winning the prize for grossest colony, don't you?" he asks.

"Definitely."

As we walk back to the classroom I see our assistant principal, Mr. Scott, walking toward us.

"Ms. Prince," he says, looking directly at me. "I've just been to your classroom. I need you to come with me, please."

Uh-oh.

"Oh, uh . . . okay, sure," I say, trying to hide the panic that has risen in my chest. "I'll see you in a little bit," I say to Preston.

"Yeah, I'll get this on the agar plate. Don't worry," Preston replies, looking at me with comforting eyes. For some reason, I don't think it was the dirty swab he was telling me not to worry about.

I walk behind Mr. Scott to the office. I feel very, very small as I do so. He must be seven feet tall, and his gray suit seems a bit too short for him. I can see his purple socks sticking out from under his slacks with each step. I can guess why he wants to talk to me, so I try to come up with a good excuse, but I'm too freaked out to think straight. I have *never* been in trouble. Never, ever.

He invites me into his office and gestures for me to take a seat. I do, and he sits down in his large swivel chair, a giant wooden desk between us. He's a very severe looking man, who I have never seen smile. The back of my jaw feels tight, my ears feel like they're about to melt off my head.

"Ms. Prince, do you know what our attendance policy is here at Blossom View?" he asks patronizingly.

"Yes, sir," I respond, though I don't tell him what it is just in case I'm wrong. I know the attendance policy well, but since he's the one who enacted it, I know any error I say will be immediately corrected.

"Good. So you must know that you are only allowed three absences in a quarter, yes?"

I nod, swallowing hard.

"And how many absences have you acquired so far this quarter?"

"Um, I think four," I respond truthfully: the three days from last week combined with the day I missed right after Spring Break due to a particularly sore throat.

"You're right. You have four this quarter, and we still have a few weeks of school left. I'm not so much concerned with that as I am with the fact that you missed three days *in a row* last week. That's a lot of days, Ms. Prince. I think we may need to place you in after school detention so you can get some work made up from the days you missed."

He pauses, and I feel the urge to defend myself, to tell him the truth; that it wasn't my fault, that my mom made me stay home to take care of Scout.

"Sir, I can make up the work at home once I get what I missed from my teachers! It wasn't my fault that I missed school, it was—"

"You are in the eighth grade, Ms. Prince. You are old enough to set an alarm and make it to school on time."

"I know, sir, and it's not that. See, my mom—"

"Don't blame your mother for *you* missing school! You're not in kindergarten anymore, Ms. Prince. It's time you start taking responsibility for your actions. You will serve your detention tomorrow after school. It will be one hour. I trust you will be able to tell your mother that you'll need a ride home afterwards. Go back to class."

I stand and walk out the door, stunned into silence. When I'm in the hallway, I immediately find the nearest bathroom and lock myself in a stall before the tears start falling. He didn't even give me a chance to tell him what happened! Why am *I* being punished when it wasn't my fault?! The anger and resentment that has been growing for my parents intensifies. They're the reason I had to miss school, the reason I'm behind in my classes, and now the reason that I was berated by the assistant principal and assigned detention! It's not fair, it's not fair!

I realize that I need to get back to class soon, before I get into any more trouble. It takes longer to compose myself than I thought it would, though. I step out of the stall and look in the mirror. My face is blotchy with bright pink patches, my eyes are swollen and still glistening with leftover tears. I splash some cold water on my face and dry it with a paper towel, trying to cool it down.

Just as I'm about to throw the paper towel away, the bathroom door opens. It's Lexi and Paisley. I can't hide my tear-stained face from them as they stride in. I look at them through the mirror as I adjust my hair, intending to pretend they're not there.

"Well, would you *look* who it is," Paisley says mockingly.

"Paisley, stop," Lexi says, as if anticipating what's about to happen. But why would she care? She's as much to blame for all of this as Paisley is.

"No, Lexi. *This* is the girl who is trying to take your crush away from you. I saw you and Preston eating breakfast together this morning, you know. What are you trying to do, hurt Lexi even more?" She's speaking to me like I'm a tiny child who got caught with her hand inside the cookie jar. I say nothing.

"Oh, so now you're not even gonna *talk* to us? What's the matter? Are you jealous of Lexi? Are you jealous that her parents actually love her enough to make sure they have a place to live? Give it up, wannabe. You've always been pathetic, just like those low-lives you're hanging out with now." She laughs. A merciless laugh. "Pretty soon you'll start looking the part too. Want me to give you the shoes that my dog chews on so you have a head start?"

SMACK!

Paisley stumbles back. My hand stings from the slap. I don't even remember deciding to do that. It's like my hand had a mind of its own. My heart is racing, my ears are ringing. I don't feel sorry that I did it. She deserved all the rage that was contained in that hit.

"WHAT THE HELL?!" Paisley shouts at me, holding her cheek. I look over at Lexi. She's standing there with wide eyes, looking back and forth from me to Paisley.

"I'm gonna get you in SO much trouble for that!" Paisley roars.

Lexi steps in.

"No, you're not," she says definitively as she pulls Paisley away from me.

"What are you talking about?! She just slapped me across my face!" Paisley shouts indignantly.

"Yeah, she did. But you were being a jerk," Lexi says defiantly. "I'm sick of you always acting like you're better than everyone else! Just calm down, okay?"

Paisley brings her hand off her face and looks at me with such malice it's hard to believe I ever called her my friend. I'm not too surprised by Paisley's actions, but Lexi's have stunned me. I didn't think in a million years she would come to my defense after how angry she was with me about Preston, and how I embarrassed her in the courtyard. Even though I was completely justified then, too.

"Paisley. You don't want to get in trouble either, do you? Because that's what would happen if you told on Jane. Just drop it and move on," Lexi says, trying to defuse her.

"Fine," Paisley says. "Just stay away from me, then. I don't want to be associated with someone like you anyway." She turns quickly and punches the door open, stalking away into the hall.

Her absence leaves a cloud of tension in the room hovering between Lexi and me.

"Um, thanks," I say awkwardly.

"No problem," she replies, crossing her arms uncomfortably. "Listen, I just wanted to tell you that Paisley's the one who found out about your family and told everyone. And… I didn't stop her. I was still mad at you and I should have made her stop, but I didn't. I'm sorry."

This is the first time Lexi has ever apologized to me, or anyone for that matter.

"Oh. Well, I accept your apology." I say this because I think it's the right thing to say, but I'm not sure I really feel it. She's been awful to me for the past several years. Now that I think about it, I'm not entirely sure why I was her friend in the first place.

Lexi smiles slightly, relieved by my words.

"Look, I really don't think Paisley will tell on you for what happened. She just needs time to chill. I'm sure she'll be fine by lunchtime, though she might not talk to you at the table," Lexi says casually.

"Oh, I'm not sitting with you guys anymore," I say quickly. I'm flabbergasted that she so automatically assumed everything would go back to normal once she apologized. Did she miss the part where I just slapped one of our 'friends' in the face?

"Why not?" she asks innocently.

"I can accept your apology for not stopping Paisley spreading those rumors, but it still happened. I don't want to be around you guys anymore. I've found some new friends. I'm sure the three of you will be just fine without 'someone like me' anyway."

I walk out of the bathroom and don't look back.

15

It's a short walk back to class. My brain and body don't quite have enough time to process everything that just happened. But there is enough time to form some conclusions. I was assigned detention for tomorrow afternoon, I slapped one of my former friends across the face, and I effectively disowned the three people who, a few weeks ago, I couldn't imagine my life without. The mixture of embarrassment, dread, and elation wash over me as I sit down in my seat next to Preston.

I need to figure out how to break it to my parents that I got detention, because they'll need to come pick me up afterwards. I'm worried that Paisley will turn me in anyway, even though Lexi is convinced she won't. And then there's an overwhelming feeling of relief that I don't have to deal with any of my former 'friends' again. I'm done with them.

"Hey, are you okay? What did Mr. Scott want?" Preston asks as he starts to put away his things. The bell is about to ring. All of that took a lot longer than I thought it did.

"Oh, um…" Do I tell him about what happened with Lexi and Paisley? I guess I should, if I've now decided he's the only friend I have. But just as I'm thinking about it, the bell rings. "I'll tell you at lunch."

He's looking at me suspiciously, and I realize that my eyes are probably still bloodshot from the tears and the rage. He doesn't say anything about them, though.

"Okay. See you then," he says, and we part ways to our next classes.

I suddenly remember that I had been planning on talking to our Science teacher about that assignment I missed. I almost turn around and go back, but decide it's not worth the effort. I'll just take a zero. Surely my grade is already high enough that it can take a hit. At least I hope it is.

After my next class, in which I was able to get a list of what I missed last week from my teacher, I head to lunch. I quickly get my tray consisting of a corndog and soggy fries, and linger a second at the front of the cafeteria until I see Preston emerge from the line with his tray. We walk together to the lunch table, where we're the first ones to arrive.

"Okay, so what happened?" Preston asks quickly, giving me time to answer before the others get here.

"Mr. Scott gave me a detention for tomorrow afternoon because I've missed too many days this quarter. I had only had one absence but then with those three from last week I was over the limit," I say briskly.

"Oh, man. That sucks," he says. "It wasn't your fault that you missed."

I feel better knowing that he agrees with me without my having to say anything. An idea suddenly occurs to me.

"Hey, do you think your mom could come pick me up tomorrow after detention and bring me home? I don't want my parents to know that I got in trouble for missing school. They'll just freak out on me."

"What's tomorrow, Tuesday? Yeah, she could probably do that. She works the graveyard shift at the beginning of the week so she'd be free. I'll ask her tonight and let you know tomorrow."

"Thank you, thank you, thank you," I say fast and appreciatively. Preston laughs through his nose.

"You're welcome. Wow, I didn't think someone could be so grateful for a ride home," he says jokingly. I can't help but grin, too.

"Yeah, well if I've learned anything lately it's that I suppose we should expect the unexpected." I look around the cafeteria as I say that, and my eyes instinctively fall on my old table. Lexi, Paisley, and Ashlynn are all sitting there, but it doesn't look like anyone's talking much. Paisley wears a scowl as she stabs her greek salad, and Lexi and Ashlynn look as though they'd rather be anywhere else.

I'm still a little lost in thought as the rest of the group arrives at the lunch table and starts eating and chatting away. I scan the cafeteria and notice a table set up along the back wall. Oh, right. That's where they've been selling tickets to the Ball.

"Jane, you alright?" Preston says to me in a low voice while the others talk about their upcoming book reports.

I break my gaze from the ticket table and look over at him. He's searching my eyes, and I can tell he knew where I was looking.

"You really want to go to that, don't you?" he asks, a bit surprised.

"Well, yeah of course, but I can't so I guess I should stop thinking about it."

"I know they talk it up a lot, but honestly I've heard that it isn't all that great," he says. "They make it seem like it's the most important thing any of us will ever go to but how can it be? It's a lame dance in a smelly gym. Not much to miss if you ask me."

"Yeah, I guess." I start eating so I don't have to talk about it anymore.

I know he must be trying to make me feel better about having to miss it, but his words just make me want to go even more. I don't care that it might be lame. I just wanted to dress up fancy and, for one night, forget about everything that's been happening. We don't have a house. My parents don't seem to want anything to do with me except to yell at me about things I can't control. My little sister is getting sick from stress. My grades are going to start falling. I got detention for the first time in my life. I lost three of my closest friends.

I sigh inwardly. A little break from having to deal with all of that would be nice. But all I can do is dream. The Earth doesn't stop turning.

"You know, if you want to, you can come with my mom and I on Friday night," Preston says. "We're serving at my church's soup kitchen. It's no fancy Ball, but it's something to do. There's always a lot of people that come. Could be fun."

Well, if I can't go to the Ball then I might as well do something with my new best friend. Even if it doesn't really sound 'fun' at all.

"Okay. Sure, that sounds good," I reply.

"Awesome. Pastor Ralph will be happy. He's always looking for more volunteers and he was getting worried about this week. Not many people have signed up to help so far." His excitement about me joining him makes me laugh a little. Not out of mockery, but out of genuine elation that my friend *actually* wants me around.

Throughout the rest of lunch, Preston's friends invite me into their conversations like I've been there all year. I finish out the school day by getting my make-up work from my teachers, then ride the bus to Nana's.

In the afternoon and evening, I just sit at the kitchen table and try to get as much work done as I can, but my brain feels foggier than usual. It's hard to concentrate, and I'm not sure why. In the past, I've been able to crank out a five-page paper in an hour. Now I'm struggling to finish a single page of math problems.

I close my math book in frustration when I can't take anymore of looking at the same graph for the tenth time. I can finish it tomorrow in detention. Oh, that reminds me. I need to give my parents an excuse for why I have to stay after school tomorrow. I put my school stuff in my backpack and go to the living room to find them talking with Nana while Scout plays on the floor. None of them acknowledge me when I come in as they're entrenched in simple small talk and can't be bothered to divert from that.

I sit down on the edge of the reading chair next to Nana.

"Preston and I are going to be staying after school tomorrow for a little while. He's going to help me with some of the work I missed last week. His mom will pick us up after. It'll only be an hour. I'll be back before dinner." I say all of this like a robot, and without prompting. What a terrible liar I am. Thankfully though, since neither of my parents were listening that closely, they didn't notice.

"That's fine," Mom says without looking at me. She returns to her conversation with Dad and Nana.

That was easy. I get up from the chair and go into the bedroom, where Scout follows me. I sit on the bed with one leg underneath me, the other dangling to the side.

"Hey, Scout," I say as she hops up onto the bed to sit next to me. "Did you have a good day?"

"Yeah!" she says quite enthusiastically. She's seeming much more like herself. "I got to play on the big playground again and then we played with chalk and then we sang songs and then…" She rambles on for a solid minute without taking a breath, telling me every single thing she did at daycare. As she speaks, I'm floored by how much she got to do. She never got to do all that stuff before now. When she stayed at home with Mom, they didn't do much. Mom did her own thing and Scout played by herself or watched her TV show. Maybe I've been wrong about the daycare. It wouldn't surprise me. My track record with my assumptions hasn't been very accurate lately.

"That's great, Scout. I'm glad you had a good day," I say when she finally stops talking. "Maybe someday I can come with Mom to pick you up. Then I'll be able to see where this awesome place is."

Scout agrees, and we spend the rest of the short time before bed playing together. Playing with my little sister used to feel like the biggest chore. But now, it makes me calm. I've been spending so much energy worrying about anything and everything, it's nice to know that I don't need to do that when we're together. Because we're both safe here, lost in a world of make-believe.

* * *

I'm sitting at our lunch table waiting for the others to arrive. I didn't see Preston this morning and got worried for a minute, but it turns out that his bus was running a little bit behind. So I ate breakfast with Stacy and Braxton. Stacy has warmed up to me considerably in just a day. I guess she's decided I'm not going to stab her in the back and has decided to trust me, at least for now.

When Preston finally gets to the table, he sits down next to me, placing his lunch tray of some sort of casserole in front of him.

"My mom said she could pick you up and take you home after detention," he says.

"Oh, great! Thank you so much for asking her," I reply.

"Of course," he says with a wry smile. "She's going to pick us up an hour after the bell rings."

"What do you mean, pick *us* up?" I ask, confused.

He sets his milk carton down that he had just taken a drink of and looks ornery.

"I may have told her that I got detention, too," he says laughing.

"What? Why did you do that?!" I ask as I laugh along.

"I just figured you might want some company. It can get lonely in the slammer."

"Oh my gosh, Preston," I say, rolling my eyes, but all the while feeling grateful that I won't be alone. "But wait, what did you tell her you did to get detention? Did she get mad at you? And won't the detention teacher know that you're not supposed to be there?!"

"Hey, slow down," he says with a chuckle. "I told her I broke up a fight between two girls but the teacher thought I was involved so I got in trouble, too. See? A noble act and I was the innocent bystander. So no, she didn't get mad at me. It helped that I had some pretty good details about the fight, though. I even said that at one point, one of the girls slapped the other across the face."

I nearly choke on my casserole. I compose myself then give him a sidelong glance.

"Oh, really?" I say, trying not to look suspicious. "That's funny."

"Yeah, it was. But I'm pretty sure the other girl deserved it. By the way, how's your hand?"

I cover my mouth quickly as I don't want to spit food all over him as I laugh uncontrollably.

"It's fine," I say once I get it together. "And you're right. That other girl *did* deserve it. How did you know about that?"

"Paisley really never stops talking, does she?" he asks.

I know he's trying to be funny, but I'm filled with dread once more. I knew it was too good to be true that Paisley would keep that to herself. I mean, if she had slapped *me* in the face, you best believe I'd be telling anyone who would listen.

"No, she doesn't. You don't think I'll get in trouble for that, do you?"

"No, I don't think she's eager to admit point-blank that she's been skipping her second period class by hanging out in the bathrooms," Preston says nonchalantly.

"Wow, you really do know everything, huh?" I say, amazed at how well-informed he always is about everyone and everything.

"Nah, people just tend to tell you things when you're nice to them. They trust you and then tell you things you didn't even want to know sometimes. It's a blessing and a curse, really."

"Well, I'm still impressed," I say. And I am, truthfully. I don't think he gives himself enough credit for how kind and caring he is. He lied to his mom and said that he had gotten a detention just so I wouldn't be alone! I mean, who *does* that? Especially for someone they've only really gotten to know for, like, four days!

Then I think about all those times at the bus stop, all those times he caught my eye across the cafeteria, or in class. All those times when we didn't say much, when I didn't give him a second thought, but he still saw me. How he still does see me, for who I am, not who everyone else thinks I am. I never want to let him go. And I hope I never have to.

16

Serving an after school detention really isn't as bad as I thought it was going to be. There's only five kids in here, myself and Preston included. I don't know why I worried about the teacher caring about who is *supposed* to be here and who isn't. She doesn't even call roll. She just tells us to work silently then sits behind her desk grading papers. Preston and I sit at a table in the back so we can whisper behind our books without her noticing. The other kids just put their heads down and look like they're trying to take a nap.

Preston and I don't talk about any one topic in particular. I'm still amazed that he lied to his mom just so he could keep me company. I don't know anyone else that would even entertain the idea of doing something like that. In between our conversations, we are actually able to get some work done. By the time detention is over, I've almost fully caught up on the work I missed from last week. Well, all except for Science. But that's okay. The notes I got from Preston will help me to do well on the exam, and that's all that matters anyway.

Preston's mom is waiting for us when we leave the school. When we hop in the truck, I'm half expecting her to be silent and sullen since we got in trouble, and now she's being inconvenienced for it. But to my great surprise, she's not. She hands us each a snack and speaks to us like it's any other day. Her voice is pleasant and soft, and when Preston starts telling her about what he did today, she actually *listens*.

I'm struck with a sudden feeling of longing, and of loss. I remember a few weeks ago when I was convinced that my parents were the epitome of caring, the pinnacle of unconditional love. It isn't until I watch how Preston and his mom interact during this drive that I realize my parents haven't shown that much interest in me in a long time. The only times we've had any conversation was for Mom to order me to do something or to yell at me, Dad sitting silently by her side while that happens. I suppose I shouldn't sulk. There's nothing I can do to change their behavior, so why am I even entertaining the thought?

We arrive at Nana's and I thank Mrs. Miller as I get out of the truck. She and Preston smile at me as they drive away. I wish I could have detention every day.

* * *

The next day at school is a boring one. There's a lot more buzz about the Ball now that it's only two days away. The teachers are having to break up more whispering than they have all year as girls chatter on about what dress they bought, who they're going with, what music they think the DJ will play. I wish they would get a life and shut up about it.

There's a really long and frantic line for the ticket table at lunch. Tomorrow's the last day to buy tickets, so they need to make sure they secure theirs now just in case a tornado rips through the cafeteria tonight, making ticket sales impossible tomorrow. They need to calm down. I can't help but daydream myself, though. I'm sure there will be plenty of other opportunities in my life to dress up fancy and escape from my life for a couple hours, but who knows when that will happen? This one's right in front of me. I know I need to forget about it, but it's really hard when the entire grade is going, with the exception of Preston and me. Even the others at our lunch table were able to scrounge up enough cash to buy themselves tickets.

Lucas and Brian made a deal with their parents that they would pay them back this summer with the money they make mowing lawns. Braxton said he asked his grandmother for an advance on his next three birthday checks, and even Stacy had been saving up her babysitting money to buy a ticket. That last one surprises me, but I guess even a girl who thinks dances are lame is bound to want to go to this once-in-a-lifetime Ball. Which it is, of course. We're never going to graduate from the eighth grade ever again.

Preston doesn't interrupt me from my daydreaming at lunch. At this point, I think he's beginning to really understand just how disappointed I am, even though I act really excited to be serving at the soup kitchen when he brings it up. I know it's going to help people, but I have the rest of my life to help people. I just want this one thing, and I can't have it because my parents didn't think to set a little money aside for anything.

I'm feeling especially low as I walk home from the bus stop in the afternoon. When I walk into the house, it's just Nana there, sitting in her chair and doing her crossword. After a quick hello, I decide to go into the bedroom and try to take a nap. The events of this week have me so drained.

When I lie down on my air mattress (there's a bunch of papers and clothes on the actual bed that I don't feel like moving), my hand slides under my pillow to support my head as I lie on my side. But as it does, I feel a sharp poke on my knuckle. I sit up and lift my pillow, wondering what just left a divot in my finger. Beneath my pillow sits a thick envelope, the corner of which being the culprit of the poke.

Confused and intrigued, I open the envelope to find it stuffed with cash. One- and five-dollar bills stare back at me. I take them out to count them and find a perfect thirty-five dollars. Exactly enough to buy a ticket to the Ball.

Where did this come from?

My question is answered as I turn the envelope over. Written on it in perfect cursive is the message: "Life is too short. Enjoy it. Love, Nana."

Nana gave me money? It has to be for the Ball because it's the exact amount I need for a ticket. But how could she know any of that? I never told her about it. I never even told my parents, or Scout for that matter! I never spoke of it in this house at *all*.

I stand up and walk out into the living room, thinking that if I'm going to ask her about it, now's the time, before the rest of my family gets home.

"Um, Nana?" I ask timidly as I stand near the hallway to the bedrooms, facing her.

"Yes, dear?" she asks, not looking up from her crossword.

"Why did you leave me money under my pillow?" I don't say anything about the Ball. I want to see if she'll bring it up herself.

"Like I wrote, life is too short. I want you to enjoy it." She pauses as she writes an answer to a crossword clue. "It's not every day you graduate Middle School, now is it?" She looks up at me over her glasses and smiles.

"You know about the Ball? How?" I ask, mystified.

"There was an article about it in the paper yesterday. Some city council candidate has a daughter that goes to your school. And she seemed to think it prudent to bully a newspaper writer into publishing a story about how she was putting up a large sum of money to decorate the gym for the occasion and pay the DJ. Like it was some version of philanthropy. She must have gotten too excited, though, because she neglected to tell the writer to edit out the part where she told him how much she was planning on charging the students to attend. Not much philanthropy in that, if you ask me."

I'm stunned.

"Nana, I can't take this. It's too expensive. I appreciate you offering, but this is your money. I don't want to take it from you just to go to a party," I say, trying to hand her the envelope.

"Well that's too bad for you, because you're going," she says, refusing to take it. "Just consider it a few birthdays worth of presents. Now take it, buy a ticket, and have fun, okay?"

"But—"

"No, Jane. What, do you have something better to do on Friday night?" she asks innocently.

"No, I guess not," I say automatically. "Well, thank you." I start to feel true excitement and joy about the fact that I'll actually be able to go! "Thank you, Nana! This is amazing, but you really didn't have to do this. Thank you!" I say with a huge smile.

"You're very welcome," Nana says. "Now go rummage through that box of your clothes in your bedroom. I asked my neighbor to pull it out of your moving van so you'd have some nicer things to choose from than what was in your suitcase."

"Ok, I will! Thanks again, Nana!" I turn on my heel and basically skip back to the bedroom. Wow! I'm actually going to the Ball! I can't wait to tell Preston!

Oh, shoot.

In the elation, I completely forgot about helping at the soup kitchen. Nana asked me if I had anything better to do and I said no. It wasn't a total lie, I guess. *I* would much rather go to the Ball than go somewhere I've never been to give some random people I don't even know food. And Nana said, 'life is too short'. She wants me to go to the Ball. She wants me to have fun. I agree with her. Life *is* too short to miss something as important as this. I can go serve at the soup kitchen some other time. I can't miss the Ball now that I have the money to do so.

As I've decided that's the route I'm taking, I stuff the money in my backpack and start rummaging through the box to find a dress that will work. I obviously can't go out to buy a new dress, but I'm sure I have something in here that will still look really nice. After several minutes of searching and pondering, I eventually settle on a light blue dress that I've worn a few times to birthday parties, but never to school. This will be perfect. Hardly anyone will know the dress isn't new.

I fold it up neatly and set it in my suitcase. For some reason, I don't want my parents to know about the Ball just yet. If either of them finds out that Nana gave me money, they'll make me give it back and then I really won't get to go. I need to buy the ticket and *then* break the news to them, since the tickets can't be refunded. Then they'll *have* to let me go, right?

I'm so excited I can hardly contain it. After all the disappointments lately, I deserve to finally have something to look forward to. Something that's just for *me*.

In the evening, my parents act like they have been lately. Quiet, on edge, tired. I hide my happiness for their sake and my own. Scout, on the other hand, does nothing to hide hers.

At dinner, she launches into an elaborate story about the puppies that were brought to her daycare today. Her eyes are lit up like stars, her eyebrows raised with glee, and her fork threatens to splatter us all with mashed potatoes as she gestures animatedly during her monologue. I listen intently and feel relieved that she's so happy. She deserves every ounce of happiness the world can provide.

After dinner, Scout and I play in the backyard until bedtime. Since it's just she and I, I don't hide my joy, and neither does she.

When we finally retire to bed, I fall asleep quickly.

I'm twirling in my blue dress in the middle of a vast meadow. The sun shines on my face as I spin, the world passing by in a blur. I stop when I see someone standing next to me out of the corner of my eye. I look down and it's Scout. But she doesn't look right. Her eyes are sunken, her cheeks are hollow. She looks like she lost half her weight overnight. I bend down to look at her, unbelievably frightened by her sudden change of appearance.

"Scout, what happened?" I ask urgently.

"You look so pretty in your dress, Janey," she says with tears running down her face. She collapses in my arms, and the world goes dark as I scream into the void.

17

Guilt. That's the first thing I feel when I wake up, but I don't know why. I remember having a dream last night, but I can't recall what it was or who was in it. I feel shaken, though, by whatever it was. I don't know if it was the dream that awoke me or the soft light that has started to shine into the room. But either way, I know it's time to get ready for school.

I get up, tension taking shelter in my shoulder blades, and go to the bathroom to take a quick shower. Once I'm cleaned and dressed, I take the envelope of money from my backpack and shove it in my front pocket. I grab one of the granola bars my mom has set on the table and walk outside to make my way to the bus stop, eating it along the way.

The whole journey to school, I feel butterflies in my stomach that I assume are a result of the anticipation of finally buying a ticket to the Ball. The lump of the envelope in my pocket reminds me that I really need to do something special for Nana, to truly thank her for her gift. I'm still in shock that she did that, especially without telling my parents. She put it directly under my pillow – she obviously meant it to be for my eyes only – or maybe she just didn't want to risk Scout seeing me get a wad of cash when she got nothing.

I begin to wonder if this thirty-five dollars in my pocket is going to set Nana back at all with her bills or something like that. She hardly has *any* money, just like us. But she wouldn't have given it to me if she didn't think it through, right? Well, my parents bought Scout and I things all these years without thinking about the future so maybe she didn't either. I don't know. I need to clear these doubts away because it's done. I tried to give it back, and she said no. She wants me to use it to buy a ticket to the Ball, and that's what I'm going to do.

Preston and I are the only ones present at our table for breakfast today. I'm nearly bursting with excitement to tell someone that I got the money to buy a ticket to the Ball, and I can't wait to tell him.

But then he speaks.

"Oh, I meant to tell you! Pastor Ralph said that another person backed out of helping at the soup kitchen last night, so he's really grateful you're coming. I told him all about you, and he's excited to meet you tomorrow. Thanks again for agreeing to help."

Crap.

I look at him, and can tell he's genuinely excited for me to come to that soup kitchen, too. And now his pastor is expecting me to come. Oh, no. How am I going to break it to Preston that I'm not coming anymore? He'll be so disappointed. I don't want to hurt his feelings, or go against my word. But if he only *knew* what happened yesterday! He'd understand, right? He said himself he knows how much I really want to go to the Ball! I don't know what to say to him right now, so I just nod, hoping my gesture of assent isn't taken to be anything binding.

"Oh, I just remembered. I need to go to the library real quick before the bell rings to drop off a book. I'll see you in class," I say as I stuff some food in my mouth and pick up my tray, leaving the table in haste so he doesn't have time to comment on my early departure.

I actually do go to the library, but I don't have any book to return. Thankfully, I only have to linger for a few minutes before the bell rings. I immediately go to my first class and am the first one to arrive. I sit in my chair, get my notebook and textbook out of my bag, then focus my brain power onto how I am going to tell Preston I can't come to the soup kitchen.

I can't lie to him. For one, he's going to see me buy a ticket at lunch. Secondly, I just *can't* lie to him. Besides the fact that he will detect it, I don't want to break his trust. He's done nothing to deserve being treated that way. I may need to just bite the bullet and tell him the truth. Sure, it'll hurt him and it'll hurt me seeing him like that, but whatever. I'm going to the Ball.

I am silently grateful that there's not much time to talk during Science, so there's not much opportunity for Preston to bring up the Ball, or the soup kitchen, and force me to tell him right now. I need the time in my next class before lunch to work up my nerves to do it. We sit quietly, fervently taking notes on the lecture our teacher is giving. It's the most convoluted topic we've studied so far and I temporarily forget about everything else while I try to understand how in the world cells are able to breathe.

When the bell rings to signal the end of class, I tell Preston I'll see him at lunch, then walk quickly out into the bustling hallway. I spend the entirety of the next class building my courage for what's to come at lunch, but I don't think it's working. I'm starting to get a stomachache, my palms are clammy, and I keep fidgeting uncomfortably in my seat. I can't even focus on whatever it is we're doing in this class.

It seems like the bell rings twenty minutes early. I begrudgingly pack up my backpack, fling it over my right shoulder, and head to lunch. I grab a tray of food, not even bothering to notice what is on it, and go to our table. Preston is already sitting down. My heart starts to pump a little faster. I set my tray down, then settle into the chair next to Preston. My discomfort is starting to become overwhelming. Preston is engaged in a lively debate with Braxton, so I have a minute to think.

I take a look around the cafeteria, at all my classmates. I remember that day a couple weeks ago when I did this same thing. I noticed all the different little groups that people had formed. Everyone had their people who created their entire personalities around the same activity, the same interests, or the same geographical location. I saw Preston's group and didn't know how to place them. I looked at my own group of friends and wondered how others saw us because I didn't know who we were either.

Now, as I look out at the different tables, I start to notice the individuals. They're probably not who everyone thinks they are. Not all the jocks are cocky. Not all the nerds are awkward. Not all the girls from ValleyRidge are snooty and judgmental and unkind. Right?

My eyes fall onto the ticket table. The money in my pocket feels like it's been lit on fire. I could do it. Right now. I could just walk up there and buy a ticket. Hand over the money and never see it again. And risk losing the only friend I have. And let down a bunch of people who just need a little help. People like me.

"Jane, are you okay? You look like you just saw a ghost." Preston's voice cuts through the sound of my own inside my head.

I turn to face him. His spring green eyes are right there. I can almost see my face reflected in them as they bore into my soul. He is the only one who has seen me. The only one who has truly helped me. The only one who knows I don't like being alone, who knows what to do to get me to laugh, who knows how much I love my sister, who knows that I am worth sticking around for. And I love him for it.

"Yeah. I'm okay. I'm great, actually," I say calmly. My heart has slowed, my stomach has untied its knots, and I feel like a new person. "So tell me more about this soup kitchen thing. I'm really excited for it."

He launches excitedly into telling me all about it: what they usually serve (pizza on Fridays), who shows up, how long it lasts, and then tells me a particularly amusing story about a little three-year-old boy who likes to pretend he's a cat. As I listen and eat, I laugh. Truly laugh. It's a euphoric feeling. A blissful feeling. And for now, I forget about the envelope in my pocket.

When I get home from school, I notice Nana isn't there. She must have had another doctor's appointment. I take the envelope of money out of my pocket and write on the side opposite of the one Nana wrote.

You're right. Life is too short. Thanks Nana. Love, Jane.

I place the envelope under her pillow in her bedroom. She'll find it tonight, I expect. I go into my family's bedroom and take the blue dress out of my suitcase, placing it back neatly inside the box from the moving van. I scoot it into the small closet in the room and close the door. There will be plenty more times to wear a fancy dress. But this is not one of them. And for that, I am grateful.

*　*　*

It's finally Friday. The day of the Ball. The school day goes by in a blur. I do my best to ignore the frenzy in the air as the vast majority of the eighth grade anticipates the evening. Preston's mom is picking us up from school today and taking us straight to the church so we can help prepare everything for the meal this evening.

As I sit in the back of Mrs. Miller's truck, I feel surprisingly content. I thought hearing everyone talk about the Ball would make me sad. And it did a little bit, but knowing that I made my decision and am sticking to it made everything so much easier to handle. When we arrive at the church, Preston gives me a hand as I hop out of the tall truck to the gravel. He leads us to a side door that gives us entry to a small gym. There's a kitchen off to the side with a big window and counter for serving. Along the back wall, there's folding tables and chairs.

"I'll see you kids a little later, okay? Preston, make sure you show Jane what to do." Mrs. Miller rubs Preston's shoulder as she walks away toward the kitchen. Through the big window I can see her greet some other women who have already started putting pizzas into one of those conveyor belt ovens.

"Right, so I always start with setting up the tables and chairs so people have a place to sit. We keep them in one half of the gym so the other half can be used for the kids to run around if they want to. Want to grab one side and I'll grab the other?" He motions to the tables.

"Yeah, sure," I say. "Okay, one, two, three!" I count as we heave the table up and walk it over to the other sideline. We do this for about twenty minutes, setting up the tables and then the chairs. When we're about two-thirds done and I'm sweating uncomfortably, I turn to Preston.

"So, do you always do this by yourself? Seems like it would take forever."

"No," Preston says grunting as he picks up a stack of three chairs. "There's usually three or four of us that do this part, but like I said, a lot of people dropped out of helping this week. Pastor Ralph was about to cancel it for tonight when I told him I was bringing someone. You really saved the show tonight."

"Oh, come on, I'm sure you would have managed," I say, blushing slightly.

"Yeah, you're probably right. I mean, how much help are you, really? You're only taking one chair at a time. Come on!" He's laughing, and tries to pick up four chairs at once and almost drops them on his foot.

I laugh at his foible. "I think I'll stick with one!"

After we've finished placing all the chairs at their tables, I look around the gym and feel proud of what we've done. I can smell the pizza cooking, and realize that I am very hungry.

"How much longer until dinner starts?" I ask Preston.

He checks his watch. "People are probably already lining up outside. Let me check with Mom and see if we can start showing people inside." He jogs over to the counter, where they've already started putting pizza onto paper plates. He comes back and reports that we can go open the door to let people in.

"Ready?" he asks.

I nod, because I am. The simple act of setting up tables and chairs gave me a sense of purpose, and I can hardly wait to see what comes next.

We go over to a set of double doors on the opposite side of the gym than the one we entered from, and open them on their squeaky hinges. When we do, I see a long line of people. It must stretch around the building because I can't see where it ends.

"Hi, everyone!" Preston says loudly so they can all hear him. The crowd says hi back in a chorus of voices and waves. "Come on in! Just make a loop around to the counter then sit wherever you like! Tonight is pizza and fruit punch!"

There's some scattered applause and cheers, and I move out of the way so the line can start moving into the gym. As it files in, I see a hodgepodge of people that I don't necessarily expect. There are people of all races, all abilities, and all ages. There are families, couples, single people, groups of friends.

I'm a little shocked when I recognize some of them. One of the first into the gym and already sitting down is the mom from the clinic: the one with the kids who were running around. Right now, they're all sitting politely in their chairs as they dig into their slices of pizza. In line is Ms. Petunia, the woman who spoke to us at the laundromat. And across the way, I see a couple of kids from Nana's neighborhood - the ones who ride my bus. I had thought everyone except Preston and I were going to the Ball, but I guess that wasn't the case.

Everywhere I look, there's people talking with one another, laughing, kids already playing on the other side of the gym. There's evidence of struggle, for sure; worn down bodies, outgrown clothing, exhausted expressions. But there's also so much joy. Eyes lit up, chatter and merriment ringing through the air. It's like an entire family…of strangers. It's beautiful.

I look back to Preston, who is looking at me. Then both of us look back out at the flock of laughter and merriment.

"See? I told you it was fun. Come on, let's get some pizza."

We each grab a slice of pepperoni pizza from Mrs. Miller. I'm just turning around to see if there's an open pair of seats when Preston suggests we go outside to eat. He leads me through the main part of the church, into one of the hallways, and we exit out of a door that leads to a small lawn on the side of the building. There's a small willow tree, its branches hanging up high enough for us to sit underneath it, leaning up against the trunk. The sun has made the sky a brilliant orange and purple, wispy clouds painting a masterpiece.

As we eat our pizza under the tree, neither of us says anything for a while. We enjoy the view, watching as the sun slowly starts to dip below the horizon. When we finish eating, we just sit there for a couple minutes, listening to the crickets and tree frogs sing their lullabies.

"Jane, I wanted to thank you," Preston says.

"Huh? You want to thank me? For what?" I ask, confused. If anyone's thanking anyone, it should be me thanking him.

"I know we've known each other for a couple of years, but these past few weeks, you've taught me a lot about what it means to overcome." A memory swirls back to me. My name. That's what it means. What my father always told me, and what I never understood. Until now.

But it still doesn't make sense, why Preston is saying these things to me. This is the exact thing *I* should be saying to *him*.

"Preston, no. I'm the one that should be thanking you. I was such a mess before all this. You're the one who showed me what it means to be kind, to be generous, and caring. *You* did that for *me.*"

He's looking down, smiling as he rests his arms on his knees.

"Well, maybe so, but I was really bitter before. I hated the way my life was turning out. I would look across the street at your old neighborhood and wonder why I couldn't be that lucky. I didn't like anyone who looked like they had a little bit of fortune because I didn't think it was fair. But I didn't know. I was ignorant. It wasn't until I really started to get to know you, Jane, that I realized things aren't always what they seem."

He pauses and wrings his hands. He looks over to me.

"Me too," I reply, looking back at him. "I realized that, too. I despised people for the things they didn't have, without realizing that I was the one who truly didn't have anything. I didn't have compassion for others. I was selfish and unkind. I'm sure I'm still a lot of those things, but I'm trying to be better."

"Jane, you're already there. You're one of the most amazing people I've ever met. Truly." I feel tears starting to well up in my eyes. Not for sadness or grief of what I've been through lately, but out of love for my best friend.

"I want to show you something," Preston says as he stands up. He walks over to an electric outlet on the side of the building I hadn't noticed before and plugs two things in. As he does, a sea of twinkly lights sparks above and around my head in the flowing tresses of the willow tree. Then a second later, music starts to flow sweetly from an old CD player on the ground. The tune is calm and instrumental. It's all so beautiful.

I turn my head to look at Preston and he's standing in front of me with his right hand lowered, the other one holding something behind his back. A bit confused, though pleasantly surprised, I take his hand and let him help me to my feet. We're standing so close I can almost hear his heartbeat. He takes a breath.

"I just thought that every Princess deserves to go to her Ball," he says quietly. He brings his other hand around and I see that he's holding a crown of flowers. Little white petals surrounding sun-colored centers.

"Daisies," I whisper, smiling.

"I thought they were fitting," he replies. He places the flower crown ever so softly on top of my head. He takes my hands and pulls me close. I feel the warmth of his gentle embrace. I hesitate just for a second before I return it, resting my head on his chest. We break apart, then start to dance; one of my hands in his, the other on his shoulder. His other hand rests respectfully on my back.

We dance to the sweet music, illuminated by the fairies' lights, lost in the unexpected paradise that is each other. I am made beautiful by his gift, by his presence, by his light. And I feel as if the Earth stops spinning, if only for a moment.

Epilogue

A letter to my teenage self

Hey there, Jane.

I know it probably feels like the Earth is crumbling around you right now. Your parents don't seem to care about what happens to you or Scout, but I promise they do. Fear and worry can make people do things you wouldn't expect, as you'll find out soon enough. I don't want you to worry, though, because everything will turn out how it's supposed to. There's a lot of life lessons we've had to learn along the way, and not all of them are easy. Friends come and go, disappointments come a lot more frequently as we age, and your childhood is gone before you know it.

Just know that you make it through this. Our family makes it through this. It's okay to let others take care of you. You don't need to be the hero all the time but go ahead if you really feel the need. Try to have some compassion for others, because you don't truly know what anyone's going through unless you've walked a mile in their shoes. Or ten miles, or a lifetime. Look for the good in every day, even if it's hard to find. Because like Nana says, Life is too short. Cherish every moment, even the hard ones, because they'll teach you more than any book can.

You are so loved, Jane. Please don't ever forget that.

Yours truly,

Jane Grace Miller

The Cost of Bliss

Acknowledgments

This novel was a bit of an experiment for me, to see if I have what it takes to become an author. As I wrote, edited, formatted, and eventually published, I understood that writing is not a solo activity. It takes the unwavering support of so many to get the words on the paper.

To my family, thank you for always lending a listening ear, for your generosity, and for your willingness to love me though it all.

To Amber, thank you for being my biggest cheerleader no matter what.

To Su, Harvey, and Bubby, thank you for being my comfort when I need it most.

To my internet friends, thank you for showing me that it is okay to be creative, silly, and unapologetically myself.

To the many libraries, coffee shops, and kitchen tables, thank you for giving me a space to tell Jane's story.

To you, a reader of my first novel, thank you for taking a chance on me, on Jane, and on her story.

There will never be enough time to say thank you enough, but I hope that Jane's story can help you to see the daisies, feel the sunshine, and dance under the lights of hope in a world that can be so dark.

About the Author

 Kelsey Conkling was born and raised in Northwest Arkansas, and happily still calls the area home. She is a Licensed Master Social Worker in the State of Arkansas, and currently works as a school social worker, serving local students and families in the public school system. She is passionate about helping children and their families recognize their strengths and develop their sense of agency to meet their goals. Kelsey has recently developed a deep passion for writing and hopes that *The Cost of Bliss* helps her readers develop greater empathy for those who suddenly find themselves in a time of need. When not working or writing, Kelsey enjoys visiting theme parks, fishing with her Poppy, playing card games, completing puzzles, singing in her car, spending time with her friends, and creating skits for the enjoyment of strangers on the internet.

If you'd like to learn more about Kelsey and follow along her journey of becoming an author, please follow her on social media: @DisneywithKels on TikTok & Facebook.

Resources

(United States)

National Suicide and Crisis Hotline: Dial 988

Child Abuse & Neglect Hotline: Check your State's reporting phone number at childwelfare.gov

National Domestic Violence Hotline: (800) 799-7233

National Sexual Assault Hotline: (800) 656-4673

United Way (Basic Needs): unitedway.org

Salvation Army (Basic Needs/Shelter): salvationarmyusa.org

Healthcare: medicaid.gov

SNAP (Supplemental Nutrition Assistance Program): fns.usda.gov/snap

The Little Free Pantries (local food assistance): thelittlefreepantries.org